PRESCRIPTION FOR LOVE

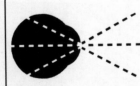

HEARTLAND HEROES, BOOK 1

PRESCRIPTION FOR LOVE

ANDREA BOESHAAR

THORNDIKE PRESS
A part of Gale, Cengage Learning

GALE
CENGAGE Learning™

Detroit • New York • San Francisco • New Haven, Conn • Waterville, Maine • London

GALE
CENGAGE Learning™

LIBRARY OF CONGRESS CATALOGING-IN-PUBLICATION DATA

Boeshaar, Andrea.
    Prescription for love / by Andrea Boeshaar.
        p. cm. — (Heartland heroes ; bk. 1) (Thorndike Press large
    print Christian fiction)
        ISBN-13: 978-1-4104-3569-9 (hardcover)
        ISBN-10: 1-4104-3569-5 (hardcover)
        1. Large type books. I. Title.
    PS3552.O4257P75 2011
    813'.54—dc22   2010050568

Published in 2011 by arrangement with Barbour Publishing, Inc.

Printed in Mexico
1 2 3 4 5 6 7 15 14 13 12 11

For my dear, sweet daughter-in-law Heather Boeshaar, an RN in the surgical intensive care unit. Thank you for graciously answering my medical questions and helping me sort out my tangled plot lines. I love you!

Special thanks to Cherie Gutkowski, a former emergency room RN and a special friend — thanks for reading my trauma scene and giving me a few pointers.

To Sally Laity and Christine Cain, my trusted critique partners for this book project. Thank you for your time and excellent comments and suggestions.

And a deep, abiding gratitude goes to my husband, Daniel, who supports and encourages me as I write.

Dear Reader,

My career in the healthcare field taught me so much. I worked in the ER (emergency room) as a registrar which gave me a unique perspective of the goings on around me. I had patient contact and worked closely with doctors and nurses, too. Pretty soon the idea for *Prescription for Love* took form. When I'd have questions, I'd wait until there was a little downtime, and then I'd ask my co-workers. They all knew I wrote Christian romance, and they were actually excited and, perhaps, even amused to contribute to the story.

As always, I love to hear from my readers. Feel free to contact me at andrea@andrea boeshaar.com.

And log onto my Web site where I write a blog called Everything Writerly. There you'll find behind-the-scenes stories about the books I've written and what the journey to see them into print has entailed. Whether you're a writer or a reader, I think you'll enjoy the blog: www.andreaboeshaar.com.

May God Richly Bless You,
Andrea Boeshaar

ONE

The late April sunshine sparkled off the blue-green water in the swimming pool and bounced off the blacktop on the tennis courts. Up in her third-floor condominium, Ravyn Woods stepped away from the window and breathed in a sigh of contentment. "What a view!"

"Yep. You've got a nice place here, sis."

"Thanks." She glanced over her shoulder at her younger sister, Teala, who had stayed overnight to help her unpack. "I've saved for a long time to buy this condo."

"I think it was worth it, although Mom and Dad are of the opinion you paid too much for your unit."

The remark didn't surprise Ravyn. She knew her parents couldn't understand her need to move out and into a home of her own. "Oh, they'll just miss my cooking and cleaning and paying rent each month."

"Yeah. Now Violet and I have to pick up

the slack."

Teala laughed and Ravyn smiled. The truth was Ravyn never minded helping with housework and paying her folks the small rental fee they charged. In fact, she often purchased groceries and stocked the kitchen cupboards. She cooked supper, too, on the nights she was home, although that wasn't often. Nevertheless, she saw to it that there was food in the house. Ravyn only hoped her family didn't starve to death now that she'd moved out of their modest home on Pennsylvania Avenue.

Grinning at her facetious thought, she peered outside once more. She stretched like a feline and appreciated the scenery below. Life couldn't get any better. But the best part would begin Monday night. That's when Ravyn would officially begin her new job as a registered nurse in the emergency room at the prestigious Victory Medical Center. It was the job she'd been striving toward for years and the stepping-stone she needed to attain the rest of her goals.

"It's all coming together," she muttered. "Just like I planned."

"Did you say something, Rav?"

"Oh, just muttering to myself." She turned from the window just as Teala reentered the room.

"I took something into the kitchen and missed what you said."

"I was just thinking aloud, that's all."

Teala continued to empty one of the many boxes strewn around the living room. "I hope you'll let me come and stay with you sometimes."

"Of course I will." Ravyn watched her sister blow a strand of tawny hair out of her aquamarine-colored eyes. "You can stay with me anytime. Violet can, too, although if you two come at the same time you'll still have to share a room."

"Oh, I plan to visit, all right," Teala said, her eyes sparkling with enthusiasm, "but are you ever going to be home? Being a nurse seems awfully demanding."

"If I know you're coming for a visit, I'll adjust my schedule."

Teala paused and regarded her askance. "Don't you think you work a little bit too much? Mom thinks so, and she worries that since you've got this condo now you'll be working more than ever."

Ravyn shrugged out an initial reply, then added, "I do what I have to do. I'm single. I don't have kids. Why shouldn't I work hard?"

"That makes sense, but — well, you might stop and smell the coffee sometimes." Teala grinned at her.

"Oh, I smell the coffee. It's the sustenance that gets me through those double shifts. In fact, I bought a new latte machine. It's around here someplace." Ravyn eyed each box, trying to recall where she'd packed her new "toy."

"What about church?" Teala removed bathroom paraphernalia from the box she continued to empty. "I'm not taking attendance or anything, but Mom and Dad are concerned because you never go to church anymore."

"I will. As soon as I get my life on track."

"When will that be?"

"Soon. I'm almost there. I mean, a few years' experience in Victory's ER and then I can apply for that research position I've been coveting at the University of Wisconsin Hospital in Madison."

"You're such a brain, Ravyn." Her sister laughed. "And you're a hard worker. I admire that."

"I just don't want to end up a charity case like Mom and Dad were all those years. A real job means money in the bank. Don't let anyone try to convince you that ministry alone will support you financially. It doesn't. We know that firsthand."

"Some ministries do."

12

"Maybe, but I'm just emphasizing what I believe. God expects us to be responsible." She narrowed her gaze. "Don't you remember how many times we went to bed hungry because Mom and Dad were waiting for God to provide our next meal?"

"That wasn't God's fault. He provided. It's just that instead of going to the grocery store, Mom and Dad spent their last dollars on paint and canvases for Dad's next production."

"Yeah, well, that won't happen to this girl." Ravyn pointed her thumb at her chest. "I never want to emulate our parents' lifestyle. They were — irresponsible."

"I agree." Teala wiped her dusty palms on the back of her blue jeans. "But, you've got to admit, people have to enjoy what they do. At least Mom and Dad have been happy all these years."

"I can't argue with that. They're like big kids." Ravyn gave her head a few wags in exasperation. She'd had to grow up fast and help take care of her family — including her parents. But her childhood hadn't been all responsibility and no play. Most of the time her fond memories overshadowed the difficulties. Her family was, in fact, very close-knit, and Ravyn felt especially grateful for her younger sister's companionship.

13

Although Teala was six years younger than she, Ravyn thought of her as a special friend.

"Hey, Rav, I forgot to tell you; I'm changing my major again."

"Again!" She shook her head in wonder. This was the third time Teala had changed her college major. "So what is it now?"

"Communications. I found out the hard way that a degree in business isn't for me."

"Well, I'm sure you can do a lot with a communications degree. It's general enough."

"That's what I thought, too." A mischievous gleam entered her eyes. "On the other hand, I suppose I could marry a millionaire and buy a house as big as this entire condominium complex."

"Sure, and you could capture a rainbow, too." Ravyn arched a brow. "You'll marry Greg. He'll continue to be a hardworking Christian day-school teacher and you'll be a professional student the rest of your life."

"Oh, you just hush. What do you know, anyway?"

"I know *you,* that's what I know." Ravyn couldn't contain a little chuckle.

Teala feigned an indignant look.

"You're smitten and that's the end of it."

Acquiescence poured over her features. "You're right. I am." A faraway look suddenly entered her eyes.

"Good grief." Ravyn sent her sister a pathetic glance. However, as Teala's big sister, she heartily approved of Greg Charney, the tall, blond, handsome young man who could easily be a modern-day John Wayne. "Teala, you're a dreamer. Just like our folks. I knew it all along."

"Hey, I have a mother who is, by her own words, a 'paintress' and a father who heads up a Christian theater group. I was doomed from birth."

"Yeah, maybe I was, too," Ravyn conceded. "But every time I think about how Mom or Dad would handle a situation, I do the opposite."

"Ooh, yeah. That's a good idea." Teala smiled and sat cross-legged on the plush carpeting. She tipped her head and strands of her golden-brown hair fell over one shoulder. "But you know what? Whether we want to admit it or not, we all have our dreams — including you."

"I have goals, not dreams. And they're all very practical." Ravyn lowered her slender form onto an adjacent cardboard box. "But what's really important to me is that I have a meaningful career and enough money to live on. I want new clothes — not raggedy ol' things that even resale shops won't sell

15

— and I can see myself driving a hot red sports car."

"With lots of speeding tickets," Teala added with a snort of laughter.

"Oh, stop it." Ravyn shot her a look of annoyance. "I just want the conveniences a woman in this day and age require for a comfortable lifestyle. In other words, I want my needs met for once in my life." She glanced around her new home. "And it all begins with this place."

"Um, aren't you missing something very important in all your *goals?*"

Ravyn regarded her sister askance. "Like what?"

"Like love!"

Her younger sister's reply haunted Ravyn for the next twenty-four hours. But, as she drove to Victory Medical Center where she'd soon begin working the night shift in the ER, she pushed aside the notion that her goals in life didn't include love. Of course they did. Every twenty-seven-year-old woman Ravyn knew wanted to get married and raise a family — including her! At the present, however, she didn't have time to cultivate a romantic relationship.

Ravyn clutched the steering wheel of her two-door compact car. The vehicle was far from the hot-red sports car that she had mentioned to Teala, but its dependability suited her needs for the time being. But someday that shiny new auto would be as real as her condo. As for love . . . Well, the sports car seemed more attainable.

Ravyn stopped at a red light. Up ahead she glimpsed the hospital's impressive brick structure, illuminated by numerous street lamps. She recalled her announcement to her family years ago that she would become a nurse. Her parents were disappointed at first. They would have preferred that she pursue something in the arts. But Ravyn knew firsthand that the term *starving artist* wasn't just a mere cliché, and she wanted more in life than to wear secondhand clothing and depend on public transportation.

Now she was in the process of attaining those goals.

Ravyn drove into the concrete parking structure connected to the hospital and pulled into a slot. She couldn't help feeling a bit nervous, even though she was confident about her abilities. She'd spent the last few years working on the surgical floor in preparation for this job as an ER nurse. Now tonight, after a week of hospital orientation, two weeks in the urgent care department, and another ten days training in the triage area, she was officially beginning the job she'd longed to do for years: work in the ER.

Entering the hospital through its employee entrance, Ravyn headed for the locker room that she shared with several other female nurses. Once she had changed into her light-blue scrub pants and a colorful printed smock top, she strode toward the ER. The soles of her white athletic shoes squeaked against an unfamiliar gleam of fresh wax that shone from the light-colored floor tiles. Sounds of a vacuum cleaner off in the distance added to Ravyn's odd feeling; she was accustomed to being here during the daytime when this hospital bustled with patients and visitors. Now it seemed — deserted.

Her perspective soon changed, however, as she walked through the emergency room's automatic doors. A kind of controlled chaos buzzed all around her, and in that moment, Ravyn felt like a lost little girl at a crowded shopping mall.

Moments later, a tap on her shoulder caused Ravyn to turn. She immediately came face-to-face with Liz Hutchinson, a veteran trauma nurse. Ravyn had become acquainted with Liz during her training in the triage area, and Liz was assigned to be

Ravyn's preceptor for the next eight weeks. The middle-aged woman had a bawdy edge to her personality, an edge that ran contrary to Ravyn's private, no-nonsense qualities. Nevertheless, Liz's nursing skills had impressed Ravyn from day one.

"Bus accident," Liz said as she snapped shut the chart she held.

"Are you kidding?" Ravyn couldn't hide her disbelief.

"Honey, I'm as serious as a blood clot." Weariness shone in Liz's blue eyes. "A tour bus was on its way back from a Wisconsin casino when the driver went off the road. Busy night — and I just happen to be working a double shift. I was hoping things would be quiet, but . . ." She glanced around. "The dice didn't roll in my favor."

Ravyn grinned at the pun, then gazed around at the numerous patients on gurneys. Some of the portable beds lined the outer wall of the ER's main area called the arena.

"No life-threatening injuries," Liz continued. "Just your typical lacerations and a few broken bones."

Ravyn nodded for lack of a better response and followed Liz's stocky form to one of the counters that ran parallel to a row of exam rooms.

"Are you punched in?"

"Yep."

"Good. I could use some help."

"Sure."

Liz sent her a grateful smile, then bobbed her head, causing the top of her short, light-brown hair to bounce. "Get *George* over there to sign these orders so we can discharge the patients in rooms 6 and 7." She slid the paperwork over to Ravyn.

"Who's George?"

"The resident over there." Liz inclined her head once more and this time Ravyn followed her coworker's gaze to where three men stood near the health unit coordinator's desk. "See the guy who looks like that actor from that hit TV show —"

"Oh, right. I see him." Ravyn had never watched the TV series, which, in her opinion, was nothing more than a nighttime soap opera, but she'd heard enough about it and read plenty of reviews. "That show is totally unrealistic. Who should know that better than you, an ER nurse?"

"What can I say? I love the drama."

Ravyn couldn't keep the grin off her lips as she regarded George. He stood not even twenty feet away from her — the man in the white MD jacket worn over light-green scrubs. He was average in height and weight, with dark-brown hair, graying just slightly at his temples. It was true; he did resemble the actor.

She froze as recognition set in. She narrowed her gaze. *No, it can't be.* She blinked. *It's him!*

"His name is really Mark but we tease him — mercilessly, I might add."

Ravyn knew exactly who he was: Mark Monroe. He'd grown up in northern New Hampshire and when Ravyn knew him, he'd loved the Lord and the theater — or so it had appeared. One summer, almost eleven years ago, he'd stayed with his great-aunt and great-uncle here in Dubuque and performed in one of her father's productions. Mark had played the lead opposite Ravyn's best friend, Shelley Jenkins. Ravyn knew her friend had fallen hard for the guy and entertained thoughts of spending the rest of her life with him. But then, after Shelley got sick with some sort of stomach flu, Dad had insisted Ravyn step into Shelley's role. She'd rehearsed enough with Shelley, and had even agreed to be her understudy, but that had merely been an excuse to hang out at the auditorium.

They'd had a lot of fun that summer, she and Shelley and Mark, along with the rest of the cast members. They'd occasionally go

21

out for pizza after rehearsals and, on a rare day off, they had attended a couple of Dubuque's riverside festivals. Ravyn had fond memories of those days, even with her little sisters, Teala and Violet, tagging along. The cast and crew never objected. Ravyn had thought of Mark as a good friend, and Shelley was her very best friend.

Then things had changed.

Shelley became ill and Ravyn had been forced to step into the lead role. Unfortunately for her, she'd dreaded being in front of an audience. Mark had spent hours coaching her, but it hadn't seemed to help. And if stage fright and flubbing her lines hadn't been bad enough, Ravyn felt she betrayed her best friend each time she acted out the last scene in which she and Mark kissed. Every time he took her into his arms and her lips met his, Ravyn's guilt had mounted. It hadn't mattered how much she'd told herself that it was a play. Acting. Pretend. She'd enjoyed it. Worse, she'd been able to tell that he had, too.

And then the worst that could happen happened — Mark broke Shelley's heart and dashed her hopes and dreams for the future. Weeks later, Shelley disappeared. Rumors circulated that she'd gone to live with some relative in Florida, but although she'd tried, Ravyn could never confirm it. Shelley's parents had refused to talk about it. Months later, they were gone, too. Obviously the situation had devastated more people than just Shelley.

And Mark Monroe was to blame.

"He hates it when we call him George." Liz's deep voice brought the present back into focus. "But that only makes razzing him all the more fun."

Ravyn gathered her wits along with the paperwork. "Which form does he sign?"

"This one — oh, and, I should warn you. George is spoken for. See Carla over there? The x-ray tech?"

Glancing across the ER, she spotted the curvy blond and nodded.

"I guess she and George are dating — at least that's what Carla told us last week when a bunch of us went out for breakfast."

"I couldn't care less," Ravyn said, "because I'm totally not interested in *George*."

Liz snorted with laughter. "Famous last words."

Ravyn scooped up the documents, walked over to the three men, and tapped George on the upper arm.

"Excuse me. Will you sign these discharge orders?"

He turned and within moments Ravyn

saw recognition spark in his brown eyes. She, on the other hand, said nothing. The swell of unresolved sadness over losing Shelley's friendship wouldn't allow any words to form.

He tipped his head. "Ravyn Woods — is that you?"

She managed a nod and hid behind her professionalism. "Hi, Mark. I need these papers signed."

"I didn't know you worked here at Victory." He took the proffered chart. "I thought you lived in Wisconsin and worked at the University Hospital."

"That's where I'm headed — eventually." Surprise loosened her tongue. How did he know that?

"Oh. Well . . ." He continued to smile at her, and she resisted the urge to squirm under his intense scrutiny. "Have you been at Victory long?"

"A few weeks."

"That explains why I haven't seen you before now."

Ravyn longed to wipe the silly grin off his face.

"It's really nice to see you again."

"Thanks."

"Ironic how we both ended up in the medical field."

"Yeah." She tapped her finger on the chart. "We're waiting on your autograph here, *Doctor.*"

"Oh. Right." He glanced down at the paperwork. "Who's being discharged?"

"Ian Jeffers and Wanda Smith. The patients in rooms 6 and 7."

Mark glanced at the white board behind him on which every patient's first name had been written. "Great. I'm sure they'll be happy to go home." He pulled his ink pen from his white jacket's breast pocket and scratched his signature across each page.

"You know, it's crossed my mind to give you a call," he said. "Aunt Edy's done her best to keep me up-to-date on you and your family. She said you lived at home —"

"Not anymore."

"Oh." He shook his head, looking embarrassed. "I haven't heard an update in a while. Med school and my residency have absorbed most of my adult life." He smiled. "And keeping up with you and your family was a lot easier when they belonged to the same church as Aunt Edy and Uncle Chet."

Ravyn figured that was probably true. At one time her family attended the same church as the Dariens. But when it grew too large, the pastor felt it became too impersonal and he developed an idea for a spin-off church on the other side of town. Ravyn's folks were always up for an adventure and volunteered to be some of those members who left to help start the new church.

"Last I heard you'd graduated from college. I even saw your picture in the newspaper."

"That was five years ago."

Mark nodded. "Like I said, I'm out of touch. But maybe if things slow down later we can talk and catch up." He handed her the sheets of paper.

She pushed out a tight little smile.

"Or, better yet, give me your phone number and I call you sometime soon."

When pigs fly!

At that instant, Carla walked by and sent Ravyn a scathing look. Ravyn's opinion of Mark slipped a notch lower. Not only was he a hypocrite and a heartbreaker, he put Casanova to shame.

Without another word, Ravyn strode back to where the patients' charts lay on the counter. She slipped the multicolored forms into the appropriate chart. When she looked up, she caught Mark's dark-eyed stare. He smiled and Ravyn quickly lowered her gaze.

"Hey, quit making eyes at George, will you?" Liz came to stand alongside her. "I need help with Mrs. Johnson in room 8."

"I'm not making eyes at anyone. That's the last thing I'd do — especially with *him.*"

"Oh?" Liz's expression said she was interested in knowing why.

But Ravyn wasn't about to divulge her personal reasons. This was her job. Her livelihood. Unfortunately, her nerves felt jangled as she carried the charts to the unit clerk's desk. The night wasn't off to the start she had hoped for. Her new position was suddenly overshadowed by a real-life drama — one she wanted no part of. A wandering-eyed resident, a loudmouth coworker, and a jealous x-ray tech.

Ravyn began to dread the next eleven and a half hours.

TWO

Dr. Mark Monroe glanced at his wristwatch. The time he'd been waiting for was now just minutes away — time to go home. He was going on twenty-four hours without a decent night's sleep and he felt exhausted. His body craved a soft mattress covered by clean, fresh-smelling sheets, a far cry from the lumpy bed in the residents' room outside of the intensive care unit. But when Ravyn showed up in the ER, Mark suddenly felt a surge of energy. It was great to see her again; he felt like he'd run into a long-lost friend. But did he detect a hint of animosity? Maybe he'd been too forward in asking for her phone number. Under other circumstances, he wouldn't have been so bold, but he was acquainted with Ravyn and her family. Of course, Ravyn might be dating someone. Maybe she'd even gotten married.

No, Aunt Edy would have heard that news and told him.

"Hey, Monroe."

Mark gave himself a mental shake and turned to see Dr. Len Tadish, the house MD, marching toward him, wearing his ever-stoic expression. The man looked like a drill sergeant in physicians' garb.

"Baker's got pharyngitis. I need you to stay until tomorrow morning."

Mark knew better than to argue. "Okay." One more shift and then he'd be off for eight hours. Maybe it wouldn't be so bad.

The veteran physician gave Mark a friendly slap on the back. "You're covering the ER. Looks like there are four patients who need consults and you've got two traumas coming in."

"Won–der–ful." Mark didn't even attempt to conceal his sarcasm.

"Have a good one." Tadish gave him a grin and exited the ER.

Mark blew out a weary breath and reminded himself that it wouldn't be long now; he would complete his residency at the end of June. Even though he had *MD* behind his name, since graduating from med school, he couldn't have his own practice until he finished his residency. But even after he finished here at Victory, he wouldn't settle into a clinic or further his education here at the hospital. Instead he planned to travel around the country, going from church to church, gaining support for his move to a tiny country off the coast of Indonesia where he planned to work as a medical missionary. He'd join up with a team of volunteers already there making great strides in providing basic education and health services to the nationals.

Serving the Lord in a full-time capacity was one of the things he'd taken away from his time with Al and Zann Woods that summer so long ago, and he hadn't forgotten those lessons learned, even though he had long since ditched his dreams of becoming a famous actor. Pursuing his next best interest, a career as a medical doctor, had seemed more reasonable and God-honoring for him. However, there were days Mark had to seriously wonder at his decision. When all was said and done, he'd have put in thirteen-plus years of school, which included the time it had taken him to earn his bachelors degree in premed.

Nonetheless, this was the Lord's will for his life. Mark felt sure of it. He wanted to help people, not only physically and mentally, but spiritually, too. He couldn't imagine having gotten this far without his great-aunt and great-uncle, Edy and Chet Dorien. They'd opened their home on the outskirts of Dubuque after Mark was accepted to med school here at Victory Medical College, an affiliate of Victory Medical Center. Then the Doriens had funded much of his education. They said it was their way of supporting God's work.

But in spite of the financial and emotional encouragement, med school and his residency hadn't exactly been a walk in the park. It had consumed all his time and required dedication. However, the end was near. He had a month to go. . . .

His pager bleeped, announcing the first of the two traumas.

Mark drew in a breath and slowly exhaled. Looked like it was going to be one long night.

Ravyn yawned as she made her way to her car the next morning. She had concluded hours ago that working the night shift was going to take some physical adjustment. While she had worked odd shifts before, she'd never been a third-shifter on a regular basis.

As she walked down the long hallway, now filled with employees coming in to work for the day, she opened her small black purse and began searching it for her car keys. She slowed her steps while she hunted.

"Hey, Ravyn, wait up."

She grimaced at hearing Mark's voice behind her. She had managed to avoid him for the past eleven hours, even eating her lunch in the women's locker room instead of dining with the others in the twenty-four-hour coffee shop and café located on the lower level. Just her bad luck to run into him now as she was leaving.

Keys in hand, she decided to pretend she hadn't heard him and quickened her pace. But Mark caught up to her in no time. He cupped her elbow and gently pulled her to a halt.

"Whoa, Ravyn. Hang on."

Having no choice, she turned to face him.

"I just wanted to apologize if I was out of line when I asked for your number. I realize a lot probably changed over the years." He let go of her arm and shifted his stance. "For all I know you're married now with a couple kids."

She did her best to give him a polite smile and momentarily debated whether to divulge her marital status. The truth won out at last.

"I'm not married. No kids."

"Yeah, I rather thought Aunt Edy would have known about something like that." A pleased-looking smile spread across his face.

"I'm still single, too."

Ravyn couldn't have cared less and turned to walk away.

Mark took hold of her elbow again. "Want to go out for breakfast?"

She glimpsed his hopeful expression but couldn't believe his nerve. "Won't Carla mind?"

"Carla who?" A confused frown furrowed his dark brows.

Some of the decade-old resentment she still carried in her heart spilled out into her laugh. "Very good, Mark." She applauded. "It's Oscar time for you."

"Huh?" His frown deepened. "What are you talking about?"

Ravyn had wheeled around and was now making purposeful strides toward her car.

"Ravyn."

She unlocked her vehicle, yanked the door open, then slid behind the steering wheel. Before Mark could say another word, she pulled the door closed with a slam.

Mark lay in bed, staring at the ceiling. Despite pulling the shades and drawing the draperies, the sunshine still managed to seep into the room. The sounds of children playing outside combined with a neighbor's lawnmower did little to lull him to sleep.

Worse, now that he was so overtired he felt high-strung and tense.

He closed his eyes and tried deep breathing exercises. He worked to conjure up pleasant thoughts, but all he saw in his mind's eye pertained to the fast-paced hospital setting that he knew so well.

Then he envisioned Ravyn. He could picture the way her sky-blue eye shadow matched the color of her scrubs, both accentuating her pale features and contrasting with her black hair and eyes. She'd been a pretty girl when she was "sweet sixteen," and she'd matured into a beautiful woman.

Memories resurfaced and he couldn't stifle the grin that tugged at his mouth. He'd been attracted to her from the time he met her and, at first, he'd thought she was older. She'd behaved older — hardly a giggling teenager. He was twenty and when he learned she was four years younger than he, Mark didn't dare pursue a romantic relationship. But they became friends and Mark would forever think back on that summer as one of the most memorable in his lifetime. He'd looked forward to waking up each day and, except for acting out his role, he couldn't recall not having a smile on his face — from mid-June to Labor Day. Then, when Ravyn stepped into the lead role and he was actually *required* to kiss her, it had made his whole summer complete.

Mark continued to grin as he remembered Ravyn and her sisters. Each had been named after a color since their mother loved to paint. Ravyn got her name because of her dark features, Teala because of her blue-green eyes. And Violet —

Mark pursed his mouth in thought, unable to bring the reason for her name to mind. Had he ever known it?

He pondered the question a few moments before his musings came back around to Ravyn. Why did she seem angry with him? What had he done to offend her? Surely it couldn't have been the mere phone number question.

He thought awhile longer.

Bigger question yet, why had the Lord brought Ravyn back into his life?

Mark mulled over the latter. Ravyn and her family lived in the College Grandview District of Dubuque, not far from the university. Comparatively, Victory Medical Center was located west of the city and so was the newer subdivision in which Aunt Edy and Uncle Chet had built their home. Mark had always hoped to run into the Woodses. He'd even thought of dropping by for a visit since the distance between them wasn't all that far. But it just never worked out. He had practically lived at the hospital these past four years. It wasn't called a residency for nothing. Prior to that, he was in med school and that hadn't exactly been a picnic by the river, either.

He expelled a long sigh and reminded himself that his hard work would soon pay off. By the first of the year he hoped to be on the mission field.

He was so close to attaining his goals now. So close . . .

"Mark! Mark! Come quick! Hurry!"

He awoke with a start, unaware he'd even been sleeping. The sound of Aunt Edy's panicked voice penetrated his foggy mind and he bolted out of bed. Wearing a pair of gray gym shorts and a navy blue T-shirt, he left the bedroom and followed the sound of Edy's calls.

"Mark, hurry!"

"I'm coming!" He ran down the carpeted steps. "What's going on?" He fought to clear his fuzzy brain.

"It's Chet," she said, meeting him at the foot of the stairs and wringing her hands. She sounded winded and her perfectly combed and styled honey-colored hair looked almost as frantic as the light in her hazel eyes. "He was tilling the flower bed and collapsed. He's breathing, but —"

"Did you call 911?" Mark rushed past her and headed for the backyard.

"Not yet. I'll do that right now."

Mark dashed outside and across the wide, well-groomed lawn. The grass felt soft and cool beneath his bare feet. In seconds, he reached Uncle Chet, who lay on his side, his back to Mark.

He knelt over the older man who'd been a bulwark of encouragement to him the last several years. "Uncle Chet, what's going on? Can you talk to me?"

The older man groaned in reply.

Mark assessed him — pale, clammy, and his pulse beat in irregular rhythms. Uncle Chet clutched his chest and seemed short of breath. Mark guessed he was suffering a heart attack and took action at once to keep him stable until the emergency personnel arrived. Then, once the paramedics showed up, Mark stepped back to allow the two men to perform their jobs. Minutes later, they loaded Chet into the ambulance.

"Which hospital?" one of the medics asked. Tall and blond, his blue eyes sparked with intelligence and capability. Mark instinctively knew his uncle was in good hands. "Do you have a preference?"

"Take him to Victory Medical Center." Mark helped Aunt Edy into the vehicle. She had decided to ride in back where she could be with Chet. "I'll get dressed and meet you there."

She nodded and then the paramedic climbed in. The ambulance doors were closed and moments later, lights flashing and siren screaming, it took off down the street.

Neighbors stood on their front lawns and gawked, but Mark paid them little attention. He had to get to the hospital and, as much as he loved Chet, this certainly wasn't how he imagined spending his day off.

THREE

"Hi, I'm Ravyn. I'll be your nurse now because the shift changed and . . ."

She stopped short. After casting a smile, at first her patient and then at the older woman seated beside him, Ravyn caught a glimpse of Mark Monroe, wearing an apricot polo shirt and blue jeans, perched on a hard plastic chair in the corner of the ER's exam room.

She felt her body tense. Ever since their meeting last night, she had known she would run into him sooner or later. Ravyn had only wished it'd been later.

"Hi, Mark." She kept her tone polite and professional.

He sat up a little straighter. "Hi, Ravyn. Nice to see you again."

She caught his smile and decided he looked tired. "Are you on call?" She hadn't heard Mark was around, and from what she'd gathered, the buzz that *George* was in the ER usually preceded him — not that it mattered to her, of course.

Ravyn just wished she could shake him from her thoughts. She had tried to sleep today, but she'd kept reliving that summer when she'd first met Mark. She felt indignant for Shelley all over again, and the guilt that she'd been the cause of Shelley's breakup with Mark had gnawed at her for hours.

"No, I'm not on call." He nodded at the older couple. "Do you remember my aunt and uncle?"

"Of course, but I —" She opened the chart and peered at her patient's name. She suddenly felt foolish for not recognizing it at once. "I guess I didn't put two and two together."

The older woman smiled from her bedside seat. "Mark told us you that you're working here at Victory now."

"Yes. Just recently started." Ravyn decided Edy Darien had a timeless appearance, right down to her khaki slacks and hunter green cotton sweater.

"How nice to see you again."

"You, too." The reply seemed a tad automatic, although Ravyn had always thought the Dariens were warmhearted people.

"Now and then I run into your mother at

a women's retreat or seminar," Mrs. Darien said. "Are your parents doing another play this summer? I look forward to them every Labor Day weekend."

"Um, yeah, I think Dad's holding auditions pretty soon. It's about that time." Ravyn began to feel uncomfortable with the topic. She knew what was coming even before it came out of Mark's mouth.

"I had a blast that summer I worked with your folks," he said. "I'd call it a life-changing experience for me."

Life-changing is right. Ravyn decided to snip the personal thread. She glanced at her patient and strode to his bedside. Out of habit, she checked his wristband to be sure the name correlated with the one stamped on the paperwork in the chart. "And what's going on with you, Mr. Darien? You're not feeling so good, huh?"

He managed a groggy smile, having just returned from the cardiac cath lab.

Ravyn sensed three sets of gazes on her and felt oddly conspicuous. She concentrated on taking Mr. Darien's vital signs, a routine done at the beginning of every shift, and noted they appeared to be normal.

"So how much longer until I get outta here?" her patient groused.

Ravyn pulled her stethoscope from her

ears. "As soon as a bed is available, you're being admitted for observation." She peered at Mrs. Darien. "Didn't anyone tell you that?"

"Yes, but Chet must have forgotten." Mrs. Darien patted her husband's arm.

"I don't think it registered with Uncle Chet because of the cath and the meds," Mark added.

"Very understandable." Ravyn avoided looking at Mark.

"Do you think it'll be much longer before a room opens up?" his aunt asked.

"No. I'm guessing it'll happen in the next hour." Ravyn glanced at her wristwatch. "Dr. Loomis, the cardiologist, is just finishing the orders. Then once the admitting department assigns Mr. Darien a bed, a transporter will come and take him up to the floor."

Her patient drifted off to sleep before Ravyn finished her explanation. But at least he seemed stable now.

"It's a blessing to see you again, Ravyn. I feel better knowing you're Chet's nurse," Mrs. Darien said.

"Thank you." Ravyn pushed out a smile. "Well, it's back to work for me. Before I go, can I get anything for you, Mrs. Darien? Would you like a cup of coffee? We have regular and decaf. How about a glass of ice water?"

"Oh, no, dear, I'm fine."

"And I know where every coffeepot in this hospital is." Mark chuckled.

"I'm sure you do — I mean, working crazy shifts at a hospital." Ravyn shoved her hands into her smock's pockets and reminded herself she couldn't afford to appear rude. She was new to the hospital, while Mark had been a resident here for years. "Um, Dr. Loomis should be coming in any minute now."

"Thank you, dear."

"Yeah, thanks, Ravyn."

She gave both Mrs. Darien and Mark a polite nod. Then, without another word, she exited the exam room. When she reached the unit clerk's desk she let out a long sigh of relief.

The pinks of dawn streaked across the horizon as Mark stared out Uncle Chet's hospital room window. The medical center's landscape below looked almost serene at this time of morning, but in a few more hours it would be bustling with patients, visitors, physicians, medical students, and other staff.

He yawned and stretched. After his uncle

43

had been moved to the cardiac wing late last night, Mark had driven Aunt Edy home and then returned. Now that he felt confident his uncle would make a total recovery, he was preparing to leave, too, and catch a few hours' sleep.

There was just one thing he wanted to do first: talk to Ravyn. She'd been noticeably cool and standoffish. Even Aunt Edy had mentioned it, although to her and Uncle Chet, Ravyn behaved as "polite as raspberry punch," as his aunt would say. Mark had even seen Ravyn laughing at something another nurse said. It wasn't her personality or his imagination. It was just *him*. Mark probably wouldn't care if he and Ravyn hadn't been friends and if her parents hadn't made such a profound impact on his life. But for those reasons, he felt concerned and he wanted to do what he could to make things right between them.

He checked on his uncle, who slept soundly in spite of the various ticks and hums from the surrounding machines. He gave Uncle Chet's forearm a soft squeeze and then left the room and headed for the ER.

He glanced at his watch. Seven o'clock. Ravyn was probably just finishing her shift.

■ ■ ■ ■

Ravyn hung up her smock in the tan metal
locker. She pulled off her scrubs and stuffed
them into the hospital's hamper. Next she
donned the blue jeans and pink long-sleeved
T-shirt she'd worn to work last night.
Several feet away three other female nurses
sat on backless benches and traded information about their significant others while they
dressed. As Ravyn listened, a feeling of envy
began to sprout somewhere deep within her
being. She squelched it before it took root;
she didn't have time for a love life, although
she had to admit the thought of going home
to someone who adored her seemed much
more appealing than returning to her lonely
condominium.

I'll get a goldfish, she thought with a cyni-
cal note.

Ravyn shut her locker's door a bit harder
than intended. The other nurses stopped
talking for several long seconds. She smiled
an apology and the ladies resumed their
chatter. Folding her jacket over one forearm,
she slung her purse strap across the opposite
shoulder and headed for the door.

As she made her way down the hallway,
she passed employees who were on their

45

way in to work. Suddenly Ravyn's whole world seemed topsy-turvy, from working the night shift job to the nonexistent romance in her life — and it was all Teala's fault. Her sister's favorite topics of late were her boyfriend, love, and weddings. What's more, Teala's final project for a sociology class was to interview singles and couples and to draw conclusions as to why some men and women preferred their marital status — or why they didn't prefer it.

"You sound materialistic, Ravyn," her sister had said during a phone interview yesterday afternoon. She'd called to ask questions for her project, but she didn't stay objective for long. "It's like you're putting monetary things above relationships, people."

"That's ridiculous."

"Oh? Well, when's the last time you chose to go out with friends over working? When did you choose church over a double shift?"

The inquisition stung, especially since Ravyn had been thinking about Mark and Shelley all day. With regard to her faith, she knew the Lord understood, and Ravyn even felt His love for her and His support of her hard work. But yesterday afternoon didn't seem like the appropriate time to argue with her sister, let alone tell her that she'd met up with Mark in the ER. So Ravyn kept the news to herself.

She quickened her steps down the hallway as her aggravation mounted.

"Hi, Ravyn."

Mark stood from the bench near the entrance doors and she nearly tripped over him.

"I need to talk to you."

"Um . . ." Ravyn felt taken aback by the near collision.

"It won't take long, but if you've got some time, I'd like to buy you breakfast."

Her initial reaction was to refuse the offer. Not only did Ravyn automatically dislike Mark Monroe for what had happened the summer when she was sixteen, she didn't want to get mixed up with all the drama he caused in the ER.

In the next second, however, Teala's remarks came to mind. Having breakfast with Mark would prove them — and her sister — wrong. Ravyn had always enjoyed blowing up misconceptions. As for her coworkers, she figured she could explain it away easily enough if they ever found out. After all, she and Mark knew each other long before they'd entered the medical field.

Besides, she had a few choice words to say to him, too.

"Um. Sure. Breakfast it is."

Mark looked a bit surprised that she'd accepted the invitation, and Ravyn almost laughed.

"Good." He rubbed his palms together and sent her a grin. "How about if we go over to Oscar's Family Restaurant? It's right up the block and they serve a terrific omelet."

"Okay, I'll meet you there."

While Mark took the parking structure's elevator to reach his car, Ravyn walked out to the main floor, found her vehicle, and climbed in. She decided that one benefit to starting her shift at six thirty in the evening was that parking slots were plentiful. Clinics were closed when she began working, and except for a few departments, staff, patients, and visitors had gone home.

As she drove to the restaurant, Ravyn mentally rehearsed what she'd say to Mark. Maybe she'd wait until after they'd eaten — or would it be better to tell him what a jerk he was right away and get it over with?

She found the small eatery without any trouble and drove into its crowded asphalt lot. After circling twice, she finally saw a vacant slot and parked.

Her fingers curled around the gray steering wheel as she, once again, went over her list of grievances. Then a soft tap on her window gave her a start, and Mark Monroe's grinning face peered through the glass.

Ravyn sucked in a breath and gathered her resolve. There was no turning back now.

FOUR

Ravyn sipped her coffee and decided it was the best brew she'd tasted in a long time.

"This place makes dynamite coffee," Mark stated, as if divining her very thoughts. "But don't plan on sleeping anytime soon after drinking it."

"I don't work for the next two nights, so I'll be okay."

"Work the weekend?"

Ravyn nodded and eyed the menu.

"I don't think I've had a weekend off in five years." Mark chuckled. "Med school was four years. My residency another three —"

Okay, it's time. She slapped the menu closed and stared across the table at him. "What do you need to speak to me about?" She suddenly saw no purpose in the polite small talk they'd engaged in since entering the restaurant.

Mark pursed his lips and sent her a glance.

Then he, too, closed his menu. "I just wondered if you're all right."

"Me?" She raised her eyebrows.

He nodded.

Before Ravyn could answer, the waitress appeared.

Mark ordered for the both of them. "Two of your Greek omelets with the works."

The chubby brunette in her brown polyester uniform nodded and collected the laminated menus before hurrying from the table.

Ravyn couldn't contain her annoyance a moment more. "You've got a lot of nerve. How do you know I'll eat a Greek omelet with the works? For all you know I could be allergic to eggs."

Mark tipped his head. "Are you?"

"No, but —"

"Then it's all good. And you've got to try these omelets."

Ravyn bristled.

"Hey, why are you so angry? You look furious." Mark leaned forward, placing his forearms on the table. He still wore the apricot polo shirt from yesterday, and the bright color defined his swarthy features all the more. "Are you mad at me — or the whole world?"

"I'm not angry. But you're an egomaniac."

"Ah." He bobbed his head. "So it is me. I rather thought so."

"See what I mean? It's all about you. You're arrogant."

Mark actually grinned. "I'd like to think I'm just confident, Ravyn. How else could I have made it through med school? Those who doubt their abilities drop out before they even get to their clinicals."

"You say confidence. I say arrogance. Let's call the whole thing off."

Mark obviously recognized her parody of the 1937 Gershwin song and laughed. Could it be that he actually recalled how her father liked to play Gershwin's music during rehearsal breaks? The quip had rolled off her tongue without a single thought, but now Ravyn felt somewhat taken aback by Mark's reaction.

"I always appreciated your sarcastic wit."

"Whatever."

Ravyn worked at regaining her momentum while Mark took another long drink from the cream-colored stoneware mug.

"So are you dating anyone? If you are, he's one lucky dude."

"Mark, false flattery will get you to zero with me. In other words, I'm not impressed."

He held up his hands in surrender. "Okay,

okay. I'll try to remember that in the future. Except, I meant every word. He *is* lucky."

Ravyn didn't bother correcting him. Talk about *zero!* He probably sweet-talked his way through med school, too.

"As I recall, you're a lot of fun. You used to get me laughing so hard I couldn't stop. Remember that Sunday morning in church? I thought your dad was going to have a conniption because the two of us laughed so hard we shook the entire pew."

"The three of us."

"I beg your pardon?" Mark's brows drew together in a puzzled frown.

The moment she'd been waiting for was at hand. "There were three of us sitting together that morning. It was you, me, *and Shelley.*"

Mark turned momentarily pensive. "Shelley? Shelley who?"

Ravyn clenched her jaw. He claimed not to know Carla at work and now he doesn't remember Shelley? What a rat!

"Shelley Jenkins. She was my best friend and *your* leading lady in the play."

"Oh — okay. I kind of remember her now." Mark wore a pensive expression as he probed his recollections. "But I couldn't say for sure if Shelley was there in church with us or not."

"She was." How could his memory be so hazy? "And she was at the carnival, too. Don't you remember how all of us, cast and crew, persuaded my dad to let us out of rehearsal early one Saturday so we could go to the summer carnival? I'll never forget it. My father has never been easily swayed — but he was that day."

"Oh, yeah, the carnival. That was a lot of fun." He smiled. "We were good friends, Ravyn. That's why I don't understand —"

"For your information, I spent that entire summer before my senior year in high school, listening to my best friend talk about how in love with you she was."

"Oh?"

"Yeah." She sent him an appalled glance. "And don't look so pleased. Your ego is showing again."

"I'm not wallowing in pleasure at the news. I'm surprised." Mark lowered his voice. "I had no idea. Give me a break, will you? I didn't know Shelley, other than she was my leading lady until you stepped into the role."

Ravyn thought it over, summoning up the countless stories she'd heard about Mark from her former best friend. He'd held her hand, kissed her — said he loved her. How could he not remember Shelley?

"You're lying — there is no point in continuing this conversation." She slid out of the padded vinyl booth and took a step toward the restaurant's door.

Mark caught her wrist. "On my honor as a Christian, I swear I'm telling the truth." He inclined his head toward the place where she'd been sitting. "Why don't you sit back down? Please. Let's get this straightened out once and for all."

Ravyn pulled out of his grasp, then glanced around the restaurant. She noticed curious stares from people she thought she recognized. Did they work at Victory, too? The last thing she wanted to do was add another link to the gossip chain. She sat back down and tried to muster a bit of dignity.

"I've always been fond of you, Ravyn," Mark said in a whispered voice, "and your parents had a huge impact on my walk with Christ. It really hurts to find out that you've harbored such resentment against me all these years."

She didn't reply but smoothed the paper napkin back over her lap.

"Please believe me when I say there was nothing between Shelley and me."

"And I suppose that means nothing's going on between you and Carla, either?"

"Carla?" A look of puzzlement spread across his face. "Who in the world is that?"

Ravyn tossed a glance at the ceiling. "The x-ray tech in the ER? Are you going to tell me you don't know her, either?"

"No, I don't, and that's the honest truth." He seemed so sincere, but was it an act?

Mark stared into his coffee cup. "My rotation in the ER hasn't been easy. It really irks me when the nurses call me George. I want my life to emulate the Lord Jesus Christ's, not some doctor on a TV drama." He looked up. "When I saw you a few days ago, Ravyn, I felt like God brought me an ally. I'm sorry to see that I was wrong."

Ravyn folded her arms and pressed her lips together, refusing to be swayed by guilt.

"But maybe we could start over." He took a sip of coffee. "Look, if I broke Shelley's heart it was unintentional, I assure you."

Their food arrived before Ravyn could answer. After the waitress walked away, Mark asked the blessing on their meal. His simple prayer somehow reached through her animosity and touched her soul. *He can't be a fake.*

"Amen."

Ravyn looked up to see Mark lift his fork and dig into his omelet. Bite after bite, he ate with a mix of haste and gusto, like a man accustomed to living his life on the run.

Meanwhile, Ravyn began to concede. She supposed it was her Christian duty to forgive and forget. Shelley was long gone; Ravyn hadn't seen or heard from her in more than ten years.

"So what do you think?" he asked. "Can we leave the past behind us and move on?"

"I guess so." Ravyn took a bit of her omelet, enjoying the rich flavor. She chewed and swallowed. "I sense that what you're saying is true, but — it's just hard for me to believe Shelley lied. She was my best friend. She told me about the two of you." Ravyn cleared her throat. "Up in the balcony. Does that ring a bell?"

Mark's jaw dropped, and judging from his expression of disbelief, Ravyn deduced the episode never occurred.

Shelley lied to me. The stark reality numbed Ravyn from head to toe. *She lied to me!*

Mark leaned forward, his gaze sharp and narrow. "Are you accusing me of some sort of misconduct?"

"No." She rescinded. After all, she had no proof. How could she, in all fairness, hurl such profound allegations at him based on what she recalled hearing at age sixteen? "No, and I'm sorry. I shouldn't have said what I did. I get the distinct feeling Shelley fabricated the romance between herself and you."

"That's some heavy-duty fabrication." Mark sat back. "Maybe I should have a talk with her."

"Good idea. If you can find her. I haven't seen her since she left Dubuque almost eleven years ago."

"What?" He looked both perplexed and amused. "And you've been mad at me all this time? For nothing?"

Humiliation, confusion, and remorse converged inside her heart. "Well, it's not as if I thought about it night and day. I didn't."

"It was over ten years ago!"

Ravyn lifted her chin. "If what Shelley had told me was true, which I now realize wasn't, then I had good reason to dislike you."

Mark held up his hand, palm-side out. "All right. You've made your point."

Ravyn mentally groped to make sense of it all. Then she ended up spilling out the story to Mark.

"So I always felt responsible," she stated at last.

"Because Shelley got sick and you stepped into her role?" He shook his head. "You had no control over that."

"But I thought she blamed me for the failed romance between you two — the one that never existed." Ravyn massaged her temples. She felt a headache coming on.

"Hey, look, you and Shelley were both kids back then. Let's just forget it, okay?"

She nodded but sensed it wouldn't be quite that simple. What Mark didn't understand was that she and Shelley had been so close for so long it had felt like losing a limb when Ravyn lost her friendship. Shelley had left Dubuque without even a good-bye.

Mark glanced at his wristwatch. "I need to get moving. I promised my aunt I'd pick her up and take her back to the hospital."

His comment reminded Ravyn of Chet Darien's heart attack. "Is your uncle feeling better?"

"Not sure. He was sleeping when I left this morning. But I think he'll pull through just fine."

They slid from the booth and stood. Mark paid the bill at the front cash register, and Ravyn felt as though she owed him an apology. She'd said some awful things and he hadn't been obligated to explain himself, but he did. A lesser man might have lost his temper.

They walked into the parking lot, and she zipped her jacket as the cool April wind felt more like winter than spring this morning. They'd had some warm weather, but now the air had a decided nip to it.

"Hey, Mark, I'm sorry for —"

"Forget it." He pulled on his navy blue sweatshirt.

"Thanks for breakfast."

"My pleasure." He gave her a smile. "Let's be friends, all right? Life's too short for Christians to hold grudges. Agreed?"

"Agreed." She looked into his brown eyes and saw only earnestness there.

"I'll see you back at work in a couple of days. We'll talk some more then."

"Okay." Ravyn fished the keys from out of her purse, unlocked her car, and climbed in. She started her car, replaying her conversation with Mark in her mind. She believed him, although she couldn't seem to come to grips with Shelley's decade-old lies.

"Mark said he loved me, Ravyn, and right after I finish high school we'll get married. Will you be my maid of honor? I've never been so happy in all my life!"

Shelley couldn't have possibly feigned that starry-eyed gaze.

But Mark looked equally as genuine today.

Suddenly Ravyn sensed something was very, very wrong.

■ ■ ■ ■

"Hey, the place is really coming together."

"Thanks."

Ravyn bid her sister entry into the condo and closed the door. She glanced around the living room, pleased with what she saw. Her new cranberry-colored sofa with its six loose pillows had arrived yesterday, and the carpet she'd recently purchased — a woven wool blend in shades of beige, crimson, and gold — added just the right contrast. In the far corner, a beautiful oak entertainment center housed a large flat-screen TV, along with a state-of-the-art video and DVD player.

"Nice, Rav." Teala ran her hand over the beveled-glass top of the coffee table.

She felt her smile broaden. "Looks better than in the catalog, doesn't it?"

"Sure does."

Ravyn headed for the kitchen. "Would you like some coffee? I just made a fresh pot."

"No, thanks."

After plucking a large mug from the cupboard, Ravyn filled it with the rich-smelling, steaming brew.

"Hey, I'm sorry about what I said the other afternoon," Teala said, walking up

61

behind her. "I know you care about people. That's why you're a nurse. It's just that — well, Greg and I are so happy and . . ." Her cheeks pinked in a way that made Ravyn grin. "I just want everyone to experience the same *euphoria.*"

"Euphoria?" Ravyn rolled her eyes. "Good grief."

"Okay, okay. Maybe I'm exaggerating just a tad. But will you forgive me?" Teala looked at Ravyn with those wide, blue-green eyes and did a great imitation of the adorable puppy-in-the-window look.

"Of course I forgive you, but I think Greg has his hands full." Ravyn grinned before sipping her coffee. "Oh, and speaking of men, guess who I had breakfast with a couple of days ago?"

"A *man?*" Teala feigned an expression of sheer mortification.

"Knock it off, you drama queen." There was little wonder in Ravyn's mind as to why Dad cast Teala in so many of his productions. Unlike her big sister, Teala had no problem performing in front of a large audience. In fact, the more spectators, the better.

"So, do tell, Rav. Who did you have breakfast with?"

"Do you remember Mark Monroe? You

may not because you were only ten when —"

"I remember Mark. In fact, I've run into him a bunch of times over the years, but I've either been with Mom or Dad, so I just kind of stood by while he talked to them. Is that who you had breakfast with?"

Ravyn nodded. "He's finishing up his residency at Victory."

"He's a nice-looking guy — and a doctor, too?"

"Uh-huh."

"Single?"

"Yep."

Teala's eyes sparkled with possibilities. "He sounds perfect for you. A guy who's going to make tons of money."

"There you go again. You make me sound totally materialistic." Ravyn turned and strode toward the living room.

"I didn't mean it that way." Teala was right on her heels. "I just meant, well, you know. You've got, well, certain standards you've set for yourself."

Ravyn halted and Teala smacked right into her. The coffee sloshed over the mug and splattered onto the tan and off-white ceramic floor tiles.

"Oops. Sorry, Rav. I'll wipe it up." Teala traipsed to the stainless steel sink and ripped off a piece of paper toweling from the wooden holder mounted beneath the oak cabinets. "So are you interested in him?"

"No. We're friends. That's all." Her conscience pricked. If she wasn't interested in Mark, then why couldn't she shake him from her thoughts?

"Being friends is a good place to start."

"And a good place to end."

"Oh, Ravyn. Give the guy a chance."

"Maybe he doesn't want a chance. And you're a hopeless romantic."

"That'd be me."

With the spill wiped up, Ravyn led her sister into the living room where they sat on the sofa.

"The thing is," Ravyn said, sipping her coffee, "in talking with Mark, I discovered that Shelley lied to me about something that's been haunting me for years, except the incident — make that incidents — never even occurred."

"She was mean. I didn't like Shelley."

"You used to say I was mean, too."

Teala relented. "Well, yeah, but that's because you always had to babysit for Violet and me."

"The bossy big sister and her equally bossy best friend?"

"Something like that."

They shared a laugh.

Ravyn folded her legs beneath her. "I just can't believe Shelley would lie." She shook her head, thinking back on those summer days so long ago. "She'd talked about Mark all the time and she was devastated when he broke things off. But he says there was never anything between them, so there was never any breakup. I sense he's telling the truth, but that means —"

"Maybe Shelley didn't really mean to lie. Could be she was just so infatuated that she lost touch with the reality of the situation."

Ravyn had never considered it quite like that before. "Think so?"

"Well, sure. I mean, people believe all sorts of stuff that isn't true. Think about it."

"Well, yeah. It makes sense. We were both very naïve at age sixteen."

"Way back in the day."

"It wasn't *that* long ago." Ravyn sent her younger sister a quelling look.

"Long enough. Who cares anymore?" Teala made herself comfy by kicking off her shoes and setting her feet on the coffee table. "I want to hear more about you and Mark. What did you two talk about at breakfast? What kind of doctor is he? What was he wearing?"

Ravyn rolled her eyes. She had a feeling it would take some effort to convince Teala there was nothing between her and Mark. *Absolutely nothing.*

FIVE

Mark sat in the ER at a vacant workstation located between the phlebotomist's area and the unit secretary's desk. There was an incessant buzz of male and female voices all around him while telephones rang, monitors bleeped, printers and copiers hummed. He tried to ignore the commotion as he scanned the computer for lab results. A positive test meant calling and informing the patient.

A nurse leaned over him and snatched a chart off the countertop. She apologized before scurrying away. Mark barely noticed. He'd learned to tune out everything but the task at hand. However, the sudden *tap, tap, tap* on his left shoulder blade commanded his immediate attention.

He swiveled in his chair and found Ravyn smiling down at him.

"You must be really concentrating," she said. "I called your name twice."

"Sorry." He sent her an apologetic grin.

"How's your uncle?"

"He's doing well — probably go home tomorrow. Doesn't look like he'll need bypass surgery. The angioplasty seems to have been effective."

"That's good news."

"Sure is." In two quick glances, Mark took in Ravyn's appearance. The sky-blue scrubs accentuated her petite form and complemented her black hair, eyes, and thick lashes. His gaze moved over her face and he found her dark features a striking contrast to the paleness of her skin. He had to admit he liked what he saw.

"Mark?"

"Huh?" At the sound of her strong but smooth voice, he shook himself. He felt chagrined for staring. "Oh, sorry. Guess I zoned out. I'm tired." He hoped it sounded like a viable cover.

"No problem."

It worked. He expelled a breath of relief, although his reply hadn't been too far from the truth. The word *tired* could just as well replace the *MD* after his name.

Ravyn folded her arms. "When are you done with your residency?"

"End of June." He leaned back in the chair.

"Quite an accomplishment."

Mark arched a brow and couldn't help teasing her. "You sound surprised."

"No." She lifted her small shoulders in a noncommittal way, but seconds later two pink spots spread across her cheekbones. "I didn't mean it that way."

He chuckled, finding a peculiar delight in causing her to blush.

"Hey, George!"

Mark's good humor vanished and his patience threatened to follow. He glanced to his left and peered at the middle-aged nurse who'd hailed him. He abhorred the nickname but supposed he should feel flattered. After all, there were worse names RNs could call residents.

He took the proffered chart and read it while the nurse voiced her request. After scribing the order, Mark turned back to Ravyn, but to his disappointment, she'd disappeared.

When her lunch break arrived, Ravyn walked out onto what was referred to as the smoking deck. The large cement slab had been constructed adjacent to the ambulance bay and it served as a patio and smoking area for the ER staff.

Sitting down at one of the picnic tables,

Ravyn unzipped her thermal lunch bag. Next she removed the curry chicken and rice mixture that Mom created the other night. Teala had brought over a good-sized portion of the spicy concoction yesterday, and all Ravyn had had to do was heat it up in the break room's microwave tonight.

She began eating and glanced around the darkened deck. Only two halogen lamps on either side of the building provided light, but Ravyn felt safe enough. Several feet away, one male nurse whom she recognized from the ER chatted with two females while they took long drags on their cigarettes.

Ravyn regarded them as they conversed and laughed at something the other had said. A sudden pang of loneliness caused her to set down her plastic fork. She realized it was hard to be new at any job, and she welcomed the challenges this position at Victory brought her way. At the same time, however, she missed the people who had become her friends at her former place of employment. There she never used to have to eat alone.

"Mind if I sit here?"

Before she could answer, Mark plunked himself down on the bench across from her, shaking the entire table unit with his weight.

Ravyn gave him a sassy grin. "Sure, this is

public property. Make yourself comfortable."

He already had. "Just for your information, I'm not stalking you or anything," he sassed right back. "I do get an occasional break, and since I saw you sitting out here, I thought I'd keep you company."

"I'm glad you did." She smiled. "Seriously. Your timing couldn't have been more perfect."

"Good."

An awkward pause settled between them.

Then Mark leaned forward. "What are you eating? Smells good."

"It's something my mom made. Want a bite? I think I have an extra fork in my lunch bag."

"Well, maybe just a little."

Ravyn fished the disposable utensil from her gold and black-trimmed lunch bag. After handing it to Mark, she pushed the plastic container of meat, vegetables, and rice across the table.

He took a forkful. "Hey, this is pretty good." He took another bite. "Has kind of a kick to it."

Ravyn nodded and watched Mark eat some more. Deciding to let him polish off the curry chicken, she extracted a yogurt and spoon from her bag.

"Are you as good a cook as your mom?" The question came in between mouthfuls.

"I'm actually a better cook than Mom — and I don't mean that in a gloating way. But my culinary skills are well known in my family because I did all the cooking until I went to college. After that, I didn't always have time, so my sisters took turns. Mom only recently developed in interest in cooking."

"No kidding? You did most of the cooking growing up?"

"Yep. I did all the laundry and housework, too."

"Hmm."

"Mom and Dad were always gone."

"Your parents are remarkable people. They really impacted my life, particularly your dad."

Ravyn didn't reply, wondering what Mark would think if she told him how truly "remarkable" her folks had been. Al and Zann Woods had traipsed from one public housing complex to another with their daughters in tow. Ravyn remembered those years well — too well. While her parents had viewed their bleak surroundings as mission fields, Ravyn saw them as misfortunes.

"My great-aunt and uncle have influenced my life in a positive way, too. I'm the third kid out of six and I guess I always felt neglected. That's why acting appealed to me. It was an acceptable way to get attention."

Ravyn smiled.

"But your parents and my aunt and uncle helped me see outside myself and put my focus onto the needs of others."

"I'll share that with my father. He'll be very encouraged."

"Good."

Mark took another bite of Ravyn's dinner, and several moments of clumsy silence passed.

"So. Are you seeing anyone?"

She blinked. "What?"

"Any special guy in your life?"

His question made her laugh. "Mark, you're about as subtle as an atomic bomb."

"What can I say? I'm a busy guy." The chagrin was evident in the tone of his voice. "I mean, for all I know you could be in the throes of planning your wedding."

"Hardly. In fact, Teala will probably get married before I do. She's dating a teacher at Our Savior Christian School. We joke about it. Teala, the professional college student, dating a teacher."

Beneath the dim lights, Ravyn saw Mark smile. He'd left his MD coat inside the hospital and only wore his light-green scrubs. After an unseasonably warm day, the nighttime temperatures felt brisk. The ER, in comparison, was hot and stuffy. No doubt Mark came out here to cool off.

"So how come you're not married?" She figured one good inquiry deserved another. She grinned. "I should think you'd make a fine catch for any girl."

"Well, thanks. But, um, the right one just hasn't come along yet."

"Hmm." Ravyn decided he got out of answering that question rather easily.

"Actually, I dated someone on and off for a couple of years, but it became clear to both of us that marriage wasn't God's will. We broke things off and it was a mutual decision."

An image of Carla's pretty face flitted through Ravyn's mind. "Does she still work here?" She caught herself. "No, wait. You don't have to answer that. It's none of my business and I shouldn't have asked."

Ravyn finished the yogurt and reached for the red licorice she'd packed in her lunch bag. She tore open the bag.

"It's okay, Ravyn, I don't mind answering your question." Mark polished off the rice and chicken entrée and reached for a couple braids of licorice. "No, she doesn't work here. Never did."

Ravyn paused in mid chew.

"Never assume," Mark said, waving a long piece of candy at her. Then he chuckled.

"You're right. It's just that most of my friends are usually coworkers — because I spend so much time at work."

"Natural deductive reasoning on your part." Mark continued to smile as he bit off a piece of licorice. "I met Hannah at church."

"Hannah who?" Ravyn wondered if she knew the woman since she'd grown up in the same congregation. She'd only left when her folks did in order to begin the sister church.

"Remington. Hannah Remington."

"Oh, sure. I graduated from high school with Shawn Remington. Hannah was a year or two older."

"That'd be her."

Ravyn summoned up memories of Hannah. She had always won home ec awards in school and she had typically been voted Nursery Worker of the Month at church.

"You must like the domestic type."

Mark pursed his lips and raised his broad shoulders in a casual shrug. "Never really thought of it like that. I guess when the right one comes along, the Lord will let me know."

"Hmm." Ravyn made a mental note to ask Teala for the scoop on the situation. Her younger sister, it seemed, was in the know when it came to the who's who in the dating scene. Ravyn, on the other hand, was hopelessly out of touch.

She finished her piece of licorice, and while Mark helped himself to a few more strands, she reached for her apple.

"What about you? Any close calls, romantically speaking?"

"No." She mentally went over the list of guys she'd dated in the past. "No one's managed to sweep me off my feet." *Except when I was sixteen,* she added silently, giving Mark a little smile. He'd certainly accomplished the job. Of course, back then she had never purposely encouraged him in any way. She knew Shelley had her heart set on him in spite of their age difference.

Sudden memories like flood waters seeped into the crevices of her consciousness. She heard Shelley's voice in its dreamy state drone on and on about Mark. *"He said he loves me. He wants us to be together forever —"*

"Ravyn?"

She snapped to attention and glanced

across the picnic table at Mark. Could this seemingly upstanding man in the light-green scrubs be the same creep who'd devastated Shelley so long ago?

The pieces didn't fit together, but maybe Teala had been right about Shelley losing touch with reality. Perhaps that's why Shelley disappeared from Dubuque without a word — she had some kind of breakdown.

Ravyn shook off her speculation, then glanced at her gold bracelet-watch with its large round face. "I need to get back to work."

"Me, too."

They stood, and Ravyn covered and re-packed the now empty container. As a courtesy to her, Mark tossed her yogurt carton into the nearby trash bin. When he returned to the table, he set his hand on Ravyn's shoulder.

"Are you okay? You sort of spaced out for a moment and now you're awfully quiet."

"I'm fine. I just remembered something I have to do," she fibbed. She didn't want to bring up the subject of Shelley again, even though the situation continued to puzzle her.

As they made their way back to the ER, they passed Carla and another woman whom Ravyn didn't recognize. They're expressions brightened when they saw Mark, and Carla actually giggled.

"Hi, George," they stated in unison.

Ravyn glanced at Mark in time to see him incline his head, a gracious reply since he despised the nickname.

Her heart went out to him and she nudged him with her elbow. She meant the gesture to say, *Don't let them get to you,* but whether Mark understood it or not, he gave her a playful nudge right back. But his sent Ravyn halfway across the hall.

Mark caught her by her upper arm before she could trip and fall, and they both laughed.

"You're such a little thing — it wouldn't be hard for a guy to sweep you off your feet."

"You mean *knock* me off my feet."

They laughed again and continued their trek to the ER.

"By the way, that was Carla. The blond who just passed us."

"Carla?" Mark took at quick look over his shoulder. "I've seen her around."

"She's the one who apparently claims the two of you are dating."

He chuckled. "It's news to me."

Ravyn believed him. "I hate all this petty stuff."

"I do, too, but this particular third shift is

notorious for it." He gave Ravyn a smile. "Who knows? Maybe you'll be the one to change things. God obviously put you here in the ER and on this shift for a reason."

Ravyn hadn't thought of her career at Victory in that light before. She'd only seen it as fitting into her plans, not God's.

Mark pressed on the silver automatic wall plate, and the frosted glass doors to the emergency room opened.

"Speaking of the Lord, what are you doing tomorrow?" Mark paused just before they reached the U-shaped counter that encompassed the unit clerk's desk and the other computer work areas.

"Um, sleeping, I guess. I work tomorrow night."

"Can you catch a few Z's in the morning and come to the late service at church? It starts at ten forty-five." Mark grinned. "My aunt's playing the piano for a special music piece, and it wouldn't be any big deal, really, other than she just started taking piano lessons about six months ago."

"Really? Piano lessons?" Ravyn felt a smile spread across her face. She was impressed that Mrs. Darien would take on such a feat at her age. "Good for her."

"Yeah, too bad my uncle has to miss her great debut."

"Aw, yes, that is a shame."

"Well, listen, plan on coming to lunch with my aunt and me after the service. Uncle Chet won't be discharged until later tomorrow."

Ravyn felt herself stiffen. "Whoa, Mark, wait a second."

He obviously didn't hear her as the staff physician called him over. "Catch you later," he called with a backward glance at her.

Watching him go, Ravyn elected not to pursue the matter, but she'd have to tell him she couldn't accept the invitation. She had to sleep sometime and she'd hate for it to be during Mrs. Darien's solo. On the other hand, she wouldn't mind spending more time with Mark. She sensed his interest in her, but would it result in anything more than a friendship? Did she want it to be anything more than a friendship?

A vision of her condo on its lavish grounds flashed through her mind. The rest of her goals mentally surfaced, too. Her older model sedan wasn't going to last forever and somewhere there was a shiny new sports car with her name on it.

She told herself she wasn't materialistic. Rather, she was ensuring she wouldn't end up having to live with nothing, like her folks had done. The only reason they owned their own home now was because Grandpa Woods had left it to them in his will. Without Grandpa's generous gift, Ravyn sometimes wondered if her family would still be destitute.

The thought motivated her to work even harder. She picked up a patient's chart and tried to ignore the rueful weight that settled in her heart. The fact of the matter was, she didn't have time for a relationship, be it with Mark — or God.

Six

For the next two weeks, Ravyn managed to sidestep Mark each time their paths crossed. She tried to avoid talking to him unless it involved work, and she ate her lunch in places where he wouldn't think to find her. His obvious interest caused her a measurable amount of unease.

But then after Teala came back with glowing reports, having done a bit of research on her own, Ravyn felt less wary. Hannah Remington had only good things to say about Mark, although, as Ravyn pointed out, Hannah would never say a word against anyone. In addition, everyone in the ER seemed to regard him as an all-around nice guy who was honest to a fault and extremely serious about his medical career — too serious, according to some female staff members.

On a particularly slow shift in the ER, Liz and a few other RNs took delight in teasing

Mark to the point where Ravyn sensed his indignation. He never uttered a single retort, even though Ravyn knew he could hold his own if he chose to do so. Nevertheless, when her break time rolled around, she decided to seek him out in a small show of moral support.

She found him in one of the back offices where residents often studied, and knocked on the door, which stood partway open. "Anybody home?"

Mark glanced up from the thick textbook in front of him. "Hi, Ravyn, what can I do for you?"

The curt greeting caused her to feel a tad bit guilty. He had first thought of her as an ally, but she hadn't been much of a friend the last ten days.

"Want to get a cup of coffee with me?"

He actually had to think about the offer and Ravyn's regret mounted.

"Mark, I'm sorry I've been so standoffish. I . . . Well . . ."

He held up a hand. "You're learning a new job. I'm sure it's been stressful."

She didn't answer, deciding his deductive reasoning wasn't so far from the truth.

"A cup of coffee sounds good." He stood and stretched. "I could use a bit of a reprieve."

Ravyn's opinion of him went up another notch. He wasn't about to play games and that said a lot about his character.

Turning from the doorway, she stepped toward the hallway when Mark grabbed hold of her elbow.

"Let's go down the back stairwell."

"No, let's take the elevator." She'd heard taking the stairs was the long way to the coffee shop on the lower level.

"Nah, I don't want people to talk."

"I'm not afraid to leave the ER in your company, Mark, if that's what you mean."

"That's precisely what I mean." He put his hands on his hips, pushing back his white physician's coat and revealing his light-green scrubs. "Look, in a month, I'm out of here but you'll still have to work with these people."

Ravyn weighed her options and decided he had a good point. Without another word, she followed him to the exit at the end of the hall.

"I'm beginning to see why some of my coworkers have worked third shift for years." Her voice echoed in the empty stairwell. "They'd never get away with all their goofiness on first shift."

"Very true. There seems to be more of a

corporate feel around here during the day-time."

Ravyn agreed and quite frequently she found herself wishing for dayshift again instead of having to work the graveyard shift. Nonetheless, this job was the stepping-stone she needed in her career, so she'd put in her time and then make the switch once her probationary period ended.

They strode across the wide landing and down a second flight of steps.

"Just for the record, those women like you, Mark." Ravyn sent him a grin. "That's why they pick on you."

"I'm flattered," he quipped.

She laughed.

"Seriously, though, I don't want to en-courage anybody the wrong way, so it's best I keep my mouth shut. Someone's liable to get her feelings hurt and I could imagine an entire fiasco resulting."

"I suppose you're right; take the Carla thing." Ravyn opened the door and Mark followed. They left the stairway for the long corridor that led to the cafeteria. "I wonder how the rumor got started about the two of you seeing each other."

"Funny you mention that particular per-son. I discovered there's a group of people who go out after work a couple times a week and it sounds like they drink too many Bloody Marys. Carla's part of what's been referred to as the Breakfast Brigade."

"Hmm, well, boozing at breakfast would explain it." Ravyn gave him a sidelong glance. "Do you know I've never tasted a single alcoholic beverage? I saw enough drunks at the low-income housing units we lived in when I was a kid to never want to touch the stuff."

"Yeah, I don't think we're missing anything."

They made their way to the self-serve coffee carafes at the side counter, and Ravyn chose a flavored brew and mixed it with half a cup of decaf so she'd be able to fall asleep later today. Mark selected a roasted blend.

They stepped up to the cash register, and a couple of fellow residents called hellos to him and asked if he was ready for their next final exam. Ravyn felt glad she'd finished school; however, the learning process never stopped. As an RN she was required to take periodic exams in order to maintain her license. She also attended various workshops and seminars in order to keep up with the ever-changing medical field.

Ravyn slipped into a chair at a small table near some vending machines. She checked her pager. Nothing — and that meant all was still quiet in the ER.

Mark sat down across from her.

"How's your uncle?"

"He's feeling great. He's lost some weight and walks every day."

"And your aunt's piano lessons? Is she still playing?"

Mark nodded. "Uncle Chet bought her a beautiful piano. Had it delivered the other day." He raised one dark brown brow. "Too bad you missed her solo a couple of weeks ago."

"Sorry." Ravyn sipped her coffee.

"Stood me up and everything."

She laughed. "Well, if you would have allowed me to reply to your invitation, you would have known I wasn't available and saved yourself from being stood up."

"Okay, you win."

She glimpsed his wry grin before he took a drink from his tall Styrofoam cup.

Then his brows knitted together, forming a heavy frown. "You mentioned living in low-income units. I didn't know that."

"Yep. We lived in various rental units, all in rather seedy parts of the city, until I was about fifteen. Then my parents inherited the house they still live in today."

Mark pursed his lips in a thoughtful manner. "I always imagined your family living in a huge mansion — like movie stars."

"Hardly. We were dirt poor. But then my grandpa died and left my parents money. That eased our financial plight."

"I would have never guessed. Your folks are such classy and creative believers."

"Yes, they are, but class and creativity don't pay the bills and put food on the table. I believe there's a fine line between waiting on God and being plain ol' irresponsible."

A curious light sparked his dark brown eyes. "How so — if you don't mind me asking?"

"Well, either one of my parents could have gotten a paying job in between productions when times got tough. But they contended they were in full-time ministry and 'trusting the Lord.' They'd tell everyone who would listen about our needs, always insisting that 'God would provide.' Then the neighbors and church members donated stuff to us. It was like my parents were" — Ravyn waved a hand in the air, searching for the right analogy — "socially acceptable beggars."

Mark didn't reply but, instead, studied the rim of his coffee cup.

"I guess that's why I work so hard. I don't want to ever send my children to bed hungry."

He perked up. "Maybe you should work on getting the husband before worrying about any future kids."

Ravyn crumpled a paper napkin and flung it at him. "You know what I mean."

He chuckled and shot the wad back at her. She successfully dodged the hit.

He leaned back in his chair, and all traces of humor vanished. "Doesn't sound like you have a very positive opinion about people in full-time ministry."

She shrugged. "I rather think some people use the term full-time ministry as an excuse not to work a regular job. I mean, isn't it true that we're all called to *full-time* ministry if we're Christians? I guess that's how I look at it."

"I can't argue," Mark said, sitting forward again. "When Jesus gave us the Great Commission, He didn't discriminate. He's an equal opportunity employer."

Ravyn grinned and sipped her coffee. She had to admit, if only to herself, that if Jesus were her earthly employer she'd probably get fired very soon.

Lord, just as soon as I save a little more money, I'll be able to think about You and attending church again. Promise . . .

Mark flicked a glance at his wristwatch. "I think my break is over."

"Mine, too." Ravyn stood.

They walked back to the ER, exchanging amicable banter and sharing a chuckle or two.

Mark stopped in the small, unused office in which he'd been working, gathered the textbooks he used in preparation for his board exams, and sauntered out to the arena area where things were beginning to pick up. A man who'd been in a bar brawl needed his hand x-rayed, and a woman with an ankle injury was just being admitted.

Sitting down at a vacant workstation, Mark logged on to the computer. He flipped open one of the thick publications, but studying seemed impossible. He couldn't help watching Ravyn out of the corner of his eye. He wondered about her and would have never guessed she'd had a less than idyllic childhood. The Woodses always seemed like the perfect family to Mark. It pained him to hear Ravyn's parents put their ministry before their daughters' needs. But, he reasoned, perhaps that was why Ravyn made a good nurse; she'd had a lot of experience taking care of people.

She emerged from an exam room with a baby in her arms and Mark stared, half amused, half amazed. The child looked almost as big as she did. By the time he could think of forming the question, Liz, that little bulldog of a nurse, asked it for him.

"What are you doing with that kid?"

"Mrs. Rolland, in room 7, is going to x-ray, so I'm holding little Jessica." Ravyn bounced the baby on her hip. "She's almost six months old. Isn't she adorable?"

"What do you think this is, a day care?"

"No, it's night care." Ravyn laughed. "I mean, we are the *night shift.*"

"Very funny." Liz stood with her hands on her hips.

Mark grinned at Ravyn's retort and returned his attention to his book, but he surreptitiously kept an ear on the conversation. He concluded Liz was Ravyn's preceptor, and while he respected the older woman and her nursing skills, he had a hunch that she was the instigator of much of the teasing and, possibly, the rumors around here. Regardless, Ravyn didn't seem intimidated.

Then, much to his surprise, Liz was soon *gaga*-ing and *goo-goo*-ing at the baby, making little Jessica smile.

Finally, the patient was returned to her exam room and Ravyn took the child back to her mother. Mark figured he'd witnessed another example of Ravyn's care with people — babies, in this case.

He attempted, once again, to focus on his studying, but Mark's gaze kept wandering everywhere Ravyn did. He watched, fascinated, as she flitted around the ER. He noticed she did her best to exude a no-nonsense presence around coworkers, but Liz, it appeared, worked just as hard to act like a clown and make her laugh. Each time Liz succeeded, Mark had to smile, deciding, and not for the first time, that he enjoyed the sound of Ravyn's laughter.

Little by little, her personality emerged. She seemed dedicated to her job, sensitive toward the patients, and possessed a good, although guarded, sense of humor. She put up with her preceptor, after all, and Liz was a woman who thinned Mark's patience each time she called him George. But tonight he weathered the razzing so he could hang out in the arena area and continue his observation of Ravyn. In a word, he felt enchanted.

At long last, she plunked herself down in the chair beside him. "Need some help?"

"Nope."

"I don't mean to be nosy, but I don't think you've turned a single page of that textbook in the last hour."

Mark chuckled. "You're right. I haven't. I keep getting distracted." He sent her a meaningful look and she blushed to her hairline.

Conversation lagged as he regarded Ravyn and she him.

Finally, Mark scooted his chair closer to hers. He glanced around to make certain any curious nurses were out of earshot. "Hey, Ravyn," he said, his voice barely above a whisper, "how about the two of us going out to dinner sometime?"

She took several long seconds to consider his offer, but soon bobbed out a reply. "That would be nice. I'd enjoy it."

She smiled, causing Mark to grin.

Reaching into the pocket of his white overcoat, he pulled out his leather-bound calendar, containing his schedule. He opened it to the month of May. To his dismay, almost every square representing the days in that month had something scribbled on it.

Ravyn produced her schedule, too. Its cover was brightly colored and plastic-coated, and it was slightly larger than the size of a checkbook. She, also, opened to May. Doodles and appointment times filled the month. Coordinating an evening when they were both free wasn't going to be easy.

"This is going to take some doing." Mark glanced from her calendar to his.

Ravyn laughed and sat back in her chair. "I can't believe I've finally met a man whose hectic schedule resembles my own."

"Must be destiny."

"We'll see," she quipped.

Mark chuckled, but in his heart the word *destiny* rang out loud and clear.

Mark sat at the desk in the family room, tapping the end of his pencil against his textbook. Next thing he knew, the writing utensil was snatched from his grasp.

"Will you knock it off, already? You're driving me crazy."

"Sorry, Uncle Chet." Mark stared up into the older man's age-lined face. "I'm just deep in thought."

"I know, but that tapping is as nerve-racking as a leaky faucet."

Mark chuckled.

Chet tossed the pencil on the desk. "What are you thinking so hard about? Your state boards?"

"No, but I should be." He slapped the book shut. His brain had absorbed all it could for one night. Sitting back in the wooden desk chair, Mark allowed his gaze to wander around the familiar, oak-paneled room. "I'm thinking about Ravyn."

"What, we got a bird around here?"

Mark looked up at the ceiling and groaned at the wisecrack.

His uncle snorted with laughter as he collapsed onto the black leather sofa. "I've heard you mention that girl's name quite a few times in the last week or so. Pretty gal."

"I agree."

"And she had the warmest fingers out of all the nurses who took care of me in the hospital."

"That's encouraging to hear." Mark lifted his stocking feet onto the corner of the mammoth oak desk.

"Being a nurse, she'd be a help to you on the mission field." Uncle Chet paused. "Of course, I'm being awfully presumptuous here."

Mark shrugged. "It's crossed my mind."

"Just don't let yourself get waylaid this late in the game."

"Don't worry. I won't."

Mark's conscience pricked. He wondered if he'd been waylaid already. Unfortunately, he hadn't told Ravyn about his plans to move overseas. He had a feeling she'd want nothing to do with him if she knew. She didn't seem to have much regard for people who made serving the Lord their life's ambition, and Mark guessed that her spiritual walk wasn't what it ought to be. Apart from being a registered nurse, she truly was the most unlikely candidate for a medical missionary's helpmeet.

Nevertheless, Mark felt compelled to pursue her.

Compelled — or did he just feel challenged?

He looked over at his uncle, who stared back at him.

"Am I detecting a slight problem regarding a certain pretty nurse?"

"Maybe." Mark put his hands behind his head. "But I'm not ready to discuss it yet."

"Okay." Uncle Chet looked away and picked up the remote off the sturdy coffee table. He pointed it at the wide-screen TV. "In that case, I'm turning on the basketball game."

SEVEN

Another quiet night in the ER. Ravyn stifled a yawn and flipped through the pages of the Pottery Barn's most recent catalog. Her shift seemed to drag on forever when nights were slow like this. She noticed that Mark, on the other hand, relished the extra time he could spend studying. He had less than three weeks to go until he finished his residency program.

Ravyn paused to scrutinize the wood table and four matching chairs in the thick, glossy advertisement. She tried to envision Mark sitting there in her kitchen, drinking his morning coffee.

She gave herself a mental shake, realizing the direction in which her thoughts had strayed. She'd had too much time for pondering lately — and more often than not the topic of her musing was Mark.

Must be spring fever.

She stood, then strode across the nursing

station and handed off her catalog to a nurse named Betsy who had asked to see it next. Ravyn stifled another yawn and decided that, with the ER still quiet, she'd head for the lower level cafeteria and buy some flavored coffee.

She made her way through the silent hallways. Reaching the coffee bar, she selected the mocha caramel blend before heading to the cash register. She was just checking out when her pager's high-pitched, consecutive bleeps gave her a start. Several hospital staff members in line behind her chuckled when she jumped.

Finishing the exchange with the cashier, Ravyn glanced at the pager. It read: TRAUMA. 16 YOM. GSW ABD. ETA 7 MIN.

Adrenalin rushed through her body and filled her limbs. A teenager with a gunshot wound to his abdomen was on his way into the trauma center. Ravyn dropped the pager back into her pocket and, steaming java in hand, ran for the ER.

She took the steps, two by two, and when she arrived in the arena, she set down her coffee in the back of an unused work area. Next, she dashed for the trauma room — the four-bed unit, separate from the main part of the ER. A flurry of activity ensued. Residents, nurses, the staff MD, lab, and x-ray personnel were suiting up, pulling the protective clothing over their hospital scrubs.

Ravyn quickly slipped the leaded vest over her scrubs top. The weighty garment would protect her from the x-ray machines' harmful radiation. Next she pulled on a disposable gown and cap, a mask with its clear plastic eye shield, and, lastly, the latex-free gloves. She took her place at a sterile, linen-covered gurney. This was her first trauma without her preceptor's help and she wanted to do her best. What's more, Mark would take the helm under the direction of the ER's staff physician. Ravyn hoped to prove herself to him and the rest of the team.

The ambulance arrived and the patient was transported from the vehicle into the trauma room. The paramedics updated the medical team while the patient was loaded onto the gurney.

Everyone raced into action. Medical personnel pressed in around the patient, examining his wound and checking his vital signs.

Mark stood at the head of the bed, calling out orders and talking to the patient. "What's your name?"

"Jace." The name sounded muffled from under the oxygen mask covering his nose and mouth.

After the initial assessment, Mark called for the radiology staff. Everyone shifted, making room for the portable x-ray machine.

As Ravyn threaded the IV needle into the teen's arm, he moaned. Mark continued asking him questions. Where was the pain? Did he have trouble breathing? The young man answered and Ravyn happened to look up just in time to glimpse the fear in his blue eyes.

"Don't let me die," Jace eked out, staring directly at her. "Please. Don't let me die."

"We're all doing our best. Just relax." A haunting feeling descended over Ravyn's being, but she pushed it aside and concentrated on her job.

More staff pressed in around the bed as the flurry of activity continued. But moments later, the teen's blood pressure dropped. His heartbeat raced.

"We're losing him!" another nurse called out.

The patient lost consciousness.

Mark listed off the medications he wanted administered and Ravyn set to task. To assist with Jace's breathing, the staff intubated him and, finally, his vital signs were stable again. Several members of the trauma team whisked him off to the radiology department for a CAT scan, and the trauma surgeon was called.

Ravyn stayed behind and helped the other nurses with their portion of the cleanup before the housekeeping personnel came in. She prayed the gunshot wound patient would recover, and his plea not to let him die played over and over inside her head. So young — just sixteen years old. Ravyn's heart broke, not only for him but for his family. Jace was somebody's son, somebody's brother.

Oh, God, she breathed in prayer, *let him be okay.*

Back to an all too quiet ER. By now the nursing staff had learned the trauma patient's full name: Jace Lichton. Ravyn had overheard the social worker say that the young man had been involved in a fight over a girl when his opponent pulled out a gun and shot him.

As Ravyn busied herself with miscellaneous paperwork, she thought about the senselessness of the tragedy. Still, she continued to hope and pray that Jace would survive. She kept watching the clock but no news came from the surgery team.

The hours ticked by at an agonizingly slow

rate. Finally, she couldn't stand the waiting anymore and persuaded Liz to tap her resources. But even the veteran nurse couldn't find out Jace's fate, other than that he was still in surgery.

At last, the scuttlebutt that George was on his way to the ER reached Ravyn's ears. She felt herself tense, praying she'd hear something positive from Mark.

He reentered the emergency room with two other residents. Ravyn watched from the far side of the nurse's station as he shook his head — a somber reply to Liz's query.

Jace didn't make it. Tears blurred Ravyn's vision but she blinked them back. She felt almost alarmed at her show of emotion. It wasn't like her and it wasn't professional.

Drawing in a calming breath, she continued opening plastic-sealed forms and filing them on the appropriate shelves. Busywork. Something to do. But, perhaps, this sort of work was all she was cut out for. The caustic thought ate away at her confidence and soon she wondered if she'd really make an effective emergency room nurse. The surgical wing at the other hospital had been so different. More controlled and less — *traumatic.* Now she felt unskilled and ill prepared.

Mark approached Ravyn with the bad news. "Our trauma patient died in the ICU."

"I gathered as much." She cleared her throat to keep her emotions at bay, not daring to envision the sad scene with Jace's family around his bedside in the intensive care unit. "That's really a shame."

"I'll say. Only sixteen years old." Mark sat down on the edge of the desk. "Bullet nicked his aorta and —"

"Mark, please." Ravyn felt her throat tightening and held up a hand. "I don't want to know the details. We did what we could. That's all that matters."

She turned and walked away, leaving the forms spread across the work area. She had a half hour until her shift ended, and since she hadn't taken an official break, Ravyn decided to wait out her time in the women's locker room.

Once she got home she'd have a good, hard cry.

Mark yawned as he braked for a red light at a busy intersection. He'd been thinking about Ravyn as he drove home, and he sensed something wasn't right between them. Had he offended her? She'd morphed back into an ice princess and he'd thought they'd long since gotten past those cold shoulder reactions. He'd found out from other nurses that she'd been asking about the trauma patient. Was she upset about his death?

"You're home early." Aunt Edy met him at the back door.

"I start first shift tomorrow, so I've got the rest of the day off." Mark strode to the refrigerator and opened the door, looking for something to munch on.

"I made rhubarb pie."

The statement captured Mark's attention. He closed the fridge, turned, and watched Aunt Edy take a plate from the cupboard. Next she sliced a large piece of the tart treat, set it on the plate, and handed it to him. Mark pulled a fork from the silverware drawer and took a big bite of pie.

"Mmm, good stuff."

She smiled, looking pleased. "Did you get any sleep last night?"

"A little."

"What's on the agenda for today?"

"Well . . ." Mark gulped down another forkful of pie. "Uncle Chet asked me to mow the lawn, so I'll do that."

"Good. I've been worried he'd try to do it himself."

Mark acknowledged the remark with a nod. "But first I want to see if I can get a hold of Ravyn. We had a trauma last night and the patient didn't make it. I think it upset her. Could be my imagination, though, or maybe Ravyn just had a bad day, but I'd feel better if I could talk to her and make sure. Problem is I don't have her phone number, although . . ." He paused to form his plan. "I suppose I could call her folks."

"You care about this girl, don't you?"

Mark attempted a reply but his aunt kept talking.

"I've always liked Ravyn. She's a sweet little thing."

Mark just grinned.

"Sort of seems natural, doesn't it? You're a doctor. She's a nurse."

"We'll see, Aunt Edy." He laughed, partly to hide his sudden embarrassment.

"Tell you what," she continued, "if you'll mow the lawn now before Chet gets any big ideas, I'll call Zann Woods and get Ravyn's phone number for you."

"Okay, but please be discreet. I don't want to alarm the Woodses, nor do I want them to think there's more going on between Ravyn and me than there really is."

"I'll be as discreet as a church whisper."

"Oh, brother! Now I'm worried."

Aunt Edy waved off the teasing with a flick

of her small wrist. "Go mow the lawn, would you?"

"Yes, ma'am."

He moved away from the counter, but not before he saw the determined gleam enter his great-aunt's eyes. Mark guessed that she was suddenly a woman on a mission.

EIGHT

Ravyn stared out the kitchen window, over the lush green golf course. Several golf carts with white canopies puttered along the fairway. As she sipped her latte, she could hardly believe she was enjoying breakfast at four o'clock in the afternoon. But after she'd arrived home this morning and indulged in a private sob session, she'd taken a shower, then fallen into bed and slept for the next six hours. Sleeping did wonders for her mind and body, and her perspective seemed brighter, although a niggling doubt about her nursing abilities remained. Never before had she doubted herself and her future. But she kept recalling the teen's pleas to save his life, and the memory beleaguered her until she began to seriously question whether she had what it took to be an ER nurse. Maybe she didn't. She couldn't help save Jace's life, and the pain caused by that fact didn't seem worth any sort of financial gain.

Suddenly Ravyn found her goals slipping from her grasp.

The doorbell buzzed, startling her from her personal pity party. She traipsed to the door, half expecting her visitor to be Teala, so she was surprised to hear a man's deep voice resound through the intercom.

"Ravyn? Ravyn, it's Mark."

Her shock mounted. *Mark?* How did he get her address?

She buzzed him up from the secured lower lobby, only to realize she looked like a veritable slob in her oversized sweatshirt, blue jeans, and fuzzy pink slippers.

She dashed into the bathroom and gave her ebony tresses a good brushing. As she did so, she stared at her reflection. Her dark eyes looked sad and the skin below them was so transparent it almost appeared bruised. Her cheeks seemed paler than usual and, overall, she decided she resembled a drowned kitten.

Great. Just great.

The condo's doorbell chimed and reluctance weighted Ravyn's every step as she went to answer it. She opened the four-paneled door with the chain still secured and peered through the narrow opening to be sure the visitor was, indeed, Mark. Then in three succinct moves she closed the door, unlocked it, and opened it again.

"What are you doing here?"

He gave her a disarming smile. "Can I come in?"

"Sure." Ravyn opened the door wider and bid him entry. "Sit down. Make yourself comfortable."

He walked in and she shut the door behind him. She watched as he glanced around the living room area.

"Nice place."

"Thanks. I just moved in last month and I'm still getting settled."

Mark lowered himself onto the sofa and Ravyn saw his gaze stop at her pink slippers.

"Cute." An amused grin curved his lips.

She shrugged in hopes of covering her embarrassment. "Look, you can't expect much when you come over unannounced, okay?"

"I'll keep that in mind."

Ravyn ignored his laughing expression. "Want some coffee? I have a latte machine."

He held up a hand. "No thanks. I have to sleep tonight. I start first shift tomorrow and then I'm on call for the next twenty-four hours."

Ravyn sent him a sympathetic grin and

sat down beside him. It was either that or take a seat on the floor; she hadn't gotten around to purchasing coordinating furniture yet.

The smell of his musky spice-scented cologne wafted to her nose, and she noticed he looked quite appealing in his blue jeans and aquamarine crewneck sweater with its sleeves pushed up on his forearms.

She corralled her wayward thoughts. "So, um, what did you want to talk to me about? And how did you find me?"

"In answer to your last question first," he replied, still looking amused, "my aunt called your parents' house." He lazed back against the throw pillows. "Initially, I just wanted your phone number, but once I had your address, too, I figured I'd stop by rather than call."

Tucking one leg beneath her, Ravyn shifted her weight sideways, facing him. "Must be important."

"I thought so. I was worried about you. You seemed upset this morning when you left work and I wondered if it had to do with our trauma patient."

Ravyn suddenly felt as though she might burst into tears all over again. However, she hesitated to admit the fact to Mark. She didn't want him to doubt her nursing skills even though she herself was doing that very thing.

"Listen, if it's any consolation, feeling bad after a patient dies only makes you as human as the rest of us," Mark said. "We care about people. That's why we chose the health-care profession."

She gaped at him. "Are you a mind reader, or what?"

Mark chuckled. "You're easy to read."

She glanced down at her blue jeans and picked at a fray in the seam. "I care about people, but I also wanted a good-paying job. A job in the medical field seemed to fit the bill."

"Ditto."

Ravyn looked back up at Mark. Maybe they had more in common than she ever realized.

And maybe he'd be the one who would understand.

"I just don't feel like much of a nurse right now."

Mark stretched his arm across the back of the couch. "You're really beating yourself up, aren't you?"

"That kid begged me not to let him die," Ravyn said, tears clouding her vision. "I felt so helpless."

"Join the club. I was the guy calling the

111

shots. I couldn't save him, either. Nor could the trauma surgeon. But we all did the best we could." He paused before adding, "The truth is, our powers are limited."

"I know that on an intellectual and spiritual level." She expelled a weary breath. "But somehow I let my emotions get all tangled up in the incident, and there is no room for emotions in the medical field."

"True. But we're not exactly robots, either."

His expression said he related to her feelings, and Ravyn felt grateful. If she had tried to talk to Teala about this, her sister would have never been able to understand.

"You're an excellent nurse. I've seen you in action."

"Thanks." She lowered her gaze, wishing his compliment would sink in so she'd believe it herself.

"You're kind to the patients, and you endure your coworkers without complaint. The latter's quite admirable."

Catching the facetiousness in his voice, she looked up and saw him grin. She smiled at his comment, but moments later a sincere light entered Mark's dark gaze that made her breath catch.

His hand moved from its resting place along the top of the sofa, and with his forefinger, he caressed her cheek.

Time stood still. Ravyn couldn't think straight. Then Mark leaned forward and touched his lips to hers. The tender kiss made her feel heady, and it was sweeter than she remembered from a decade ago.

And on that thought her senses returned.

Ravyn placed her hands on his shoulders and pushed him away.

A little frown marred his forehead.

"Mark, is this for real or —" She narrowed her gaze at him. "Or are you just a smooth operator?"

He pulled his chin back, as if insulted, and Ravyn almost apologized. Almost. Lately she doubted everyone's motives.

She tossed the pillow aside and stood. "For your information, I'm not that kind of a girl."

As she strode to the kitchen, she hoped Mark would be offended enough to leave. Instead, he followed her, caught her wrist, and spun her around to face him. His grip was strong yet gentle, determined but hardly rough.

"For your information," he countered, "I'm not that kind of a guy."

She stared up at him, unsure of what to say.

"The truth is, I care about you, Ravyn."

With that, Mark released her wrist and gathered her into his arms. His voice was but a whisper. "Can't you tell?"

"Well, yes, but —" She felt almost dazed.

"But what?"

Within the warm circumference of his arms, all words escaped her. He kissed her again and this time Ravyn didn't push him away. But just as her knees grew weak and his hold around her waist tightened, the sharp buzzer from downstairs sounded.

Ravyn jumped.

"Whoa, a little edgy, huh?" Mark laughed and released her. "No more lattes for you."

It took a good moment for her wits to return, and she fought the disappointment that enveloped her. She had enjoyed that brief romantic interlude.

She trudged to the door. "This is probably my sister Teala."

Mark shrugged and sat back down on the sofa. "I'll consider myself fairly warned."

She grinned, but when her mother's worried voice echoed through the intercom, Ravyn felt anything but amused.

"Honey, buzz me in. I want to make sure you're okay. A doctor was looking for you this afternoon. Are you sick? What's the matter? Let me in."

"It's my mother." Ravyn glanced at Mark.

"You can escape out the patio door."

He regarded her askance. "Are you telling or suggesting?"

"Suggesting."

He smiled. "Then I'll stay. I always liked your mom."

"O–ka–ay."

She pressed the button that unlocked the lower-level entrance. Within a few moments, Zann Woods appeared at the doorway, a springtime vision in a flowing patchwork-printed skirt, white blouse, and tan, wide-brimmed hat. Ravyn thought her mom looked like she'd stepped out of a pastoral painting. The only missing element was a bouquet of wildflowers in one hand.

"What's wrong?" Zann's frown furrowed her deep-brown eyebrows. "You do look peaked. Are you okay?"

"I'm fine." Ravyn waved her in and after her mother's strappy-sandaled feet stepped into the tiny foyer, she closed the door. "You remember Mark Monroe. He's *Doctor* Monroe now."

"Of course. Hello, Mark." Ravyn watched as her mother crossed the room and headed for him with an outstretched hand. "How nice to see you again." She glanced at Ravyn, then looked back at Mark. "When Violet said a doctor needed Ravyn's address

115

and phone number, I thought . . ." Her gaze returned to Ravyn. "Well, naturally, I assumed it wasn't for a social call. I was thinking more along the lines of pneumonia or a car accident."

"No, Mom, I'm really fine."

The buzzer sounded again.

"That would be your father."

"Dad's here?" Ravyn couldn't contain her shock.

Her mother removed her hat and shook out her brown-black hair with its streaks of silver. "He was worried about you, too."

One glance at Mark's composure and polite smile told Ravyn he wasn't the least bit concerned. But as she buzzed her dad upstairs, she almost felt sorry for Mark. If the interrogation matched the one that Teala's boyfriend Greg underwent, the word *drama* wouldn't come close to describing it.

Her heart sank. After this evening, Mark might not care about her as much as he thought.

"And just what are your intentions concerning my daughter?"

"Dad!"

He laughed and gave Ravyn a juicy-sounding kiss on the cheek.

"I'm glad you're all right, sweetheart."

"I'm fine."

"And now for you, young man —"

"Oh, Dad — please. Mark is my guest."

"So I see." He grinned and stuck out his right hand.

While shaking Alfred Woods's thin hand, Mark smiled at Ravyn's obvious embarrassment. He knew the older man was just giving him a hard time. Mark could tell by the way he purposely dipped one grayish blond eyebrow.

Al chuckled. "How long has it been, Mark?"

"A long time."

"A lifetime ago."

Mark nodded. "Just about."

"Ravyn, where did you get this sofa?" Zann asked, changing the subject. She sat down, running her hand over the armrest. "I hope you didn't pay full price for it. I recently saw one exactly like this at the secondhand shop downtown. I know the manager. She probably would have given it to you for free."

Mark caught Ravyn's exasperated expression before she walked toward the kitchen.

Al stood, arms akimbo. "I think you need some more chairs in here, honey."

The last word had just parted his lips when Ravyn returned, carrying a wooden kitchen chair under each arm. Mark guessed they weighed more than she did, and he rushed to take them from her.

He set down a chair for Al, who lowered his tall, lanky frame onto the hard seat. Mark then claimed the second chair for himself. Ravyn sat down beside her mother.

"I appreciate your concern," Ravyn said, "but if you both would have called I could have saved you a trip across town."

"Guess we wanted to see for ourselves," Zann said.

"So, Mark." Al cleared his throat. "What made you decide to give up a career in theater and go into medicine?"

"The paycheck for one," Ravyn said.

Mark chuckled.

"Well, I really thought you had potential on the stage," Al continued. "And as I recall, you had a serious desire for the ministry."

"Still do. That part hasn't changed." Mark stopped short of sharing his plans to travel overseas and work as a medical missionary. But why? Was it because he feared Ravyn's possible rejection of the idea — and of him?

He regarded her as she sat curled up at one end of the sofa. She appeared so small and helpless that Mark had to fight the urge to sit beside her and slip a protective arm around her shoulders. However, he had the strong impression the word *helpless* didn't accurately describe Ravyn Woods. In spite of her petite frame, she was a capable woman.

But was she a derailment or the woman God wanted him to pursue? Mark did, indeed, care about Ravyn — more than he understood — and he sensed he was helping her over some emotional hurdles. But where was their relationship headed?

He decided that perhaps Al Woods had started off by asking the appropriate question after all: Just what were his intentions, anyway?

NINE

For the days that followed, Ravyn couldn't shake off the dark cloud of gloom that seemed to follow her everywhere she went. Her conversation with Mark had been an encouragement, and his kiss was like sweet salve on her wounded spirit. Her parents' visit had turned quite amusing as they, along with Mark and Ravyn, reminisced about that summer a decade ago in which Mark had the lead role in Dad's play. They laughed about things that Ravyn had long since forgotten, and they mentioned people she'd never forget — such as her former friend Shelley. Then, after ordering pizza, Mark suggested he and Ravyn look her up and give her a call. Make peace with the past, so to speak. Ravyn supposed it was worth a try, although she couldn't imagine when she'd have time to plan a visit, assuming Shelley agreed to it. As it was, Ravyn and Mark were still trying to free up one

Saturday night from their schedules so they could go out to dinner.

But even with those issues occupying a corner of her mind, a more recent matter weighed on her conscience: Jace, last week's shooting victim. The tragedy had affected her more than she cared to admit. In fact, she felt so troubled about it that on Mother's Day she didn't need to be begged or coerced into attending the church service with her family. She came of her own free will. Mom was thrilled.

There, in the gleaming wooden pew, Ravyn sat sandwiched between her two sisters. Their parents occupied the two places on one side of them and Teala's boyfriend, Greg, sat on the other.

Ravyn glanced at her parents. Her mother had dressed in a colorful outfit while Dad wore an outdated brown suit that looked almost fashionable again. They turned her way and Ravyn gave them a smile. For all their mistakes when she was growing up, Ravyn never doubted that her folks loved her.

She never doubted that God loved her, either. She just figured He would wait patiently for her, perfect Hero that He was, until she got her life's plan set in motion and came back to Him.

It won't be long now, Lord, she promised. *I'm well on my way to achieving my goals.*

A group of children made their way to the front of the small church and took their places on the three long steps of the altar's platform. They wiggled and grinned, and a few waved to their parents. However, they quickly donned serious expressions as the choir director commanded their attention.

The pianist began to play and the children sang.

When we walk with the Lord
In the light of His Word,
What a glory He sheds on our way!
While we do His good will
He abides with us still,
And with all who will trust and obey.

Ravyn smiled. She knew the old hymn well — as well as she knew her own name.

Trust and obey —
For there's no other way
TO BE HAPPY IN JESUS,
But to trust and obey.

The familiar and fundamental message burned within her heart. Trust and obey — no other way — happy in Jesus.

She suddenly longed for simpler days. She wished she had her younger sisters' vibrant outlooks on life. Ravyn could only recall how depressed she'd been feeling. The stress of her new job in the ER combined with the tragedy of experiencing a patient's death had depleted her courage and motivation and put a large chink in her sensibilities.

Lord, I just want to be happy again.

Then "trust and obey," she seemed to hear God say. *Don't be troubled about anything.*

Ravyn recalled the biblical command and felt led to read the rest of the passage. She lifted her small Bible and as the children began singing the third stanza, she flipped through the pages of the New Testament until she found the verses in Philippians 4.

But in everything, by prayer and petition, with thanksgiving, present your requests to God. And the peace of God, which transcends all understanding, will guard your hearts and your minds in Christ Jesus.

Ravyn closed her Bible and settled back into the pew. She relaxed her mind and made the decision to trust and obey. God was here in this sanctuary. She felt His presence. Like the scriptures taught, His arm was not so short that it could not save. God was able to steer her life back on course. She believed what the Bible said was true.

A languid peace flowed through her veins and, yes, she even felt a swell of happiness. Trust and obey.

It had been years since she'd heard God's still small voice —

And it had been even longer since she had listened.

"Hey, Monroe!"

Mark turned and waited in the hallway as Geoff Ling, a fellow resident, approached him.

"Got something for you." He handed Mark a square, white envelope. "Is it your birthday?"

"Nope." Mark inspected the handwriting but didn't recognize it.

The Asian-American doctor peered through his glasses at Mark. "One of the ER nurses gave it to me on her way out — said she was hoping to run into you last night."

Mark immediately thought of Ravyn. "I got tied up with consults."

"Too bad. She's pretty. Black hair, dark eyes —"

"I know who you mean."

"Figured you did." The guy gave Mark a friendly sock in the arm. "They don't call you George down there for nothing."

"Oh, cut it out. You know I hate that."

Geoff snickered in a good-natured manner and went on his way.

Mark tore into the envelope and pulled out the yellow greeting card. The words THANK YOU were embossed on its front. Curious, he opened it and read the words Ravyn had scribed.

Thanks for your listening ear. You were a big help in encouraging me. In church on Sunday, the Lord really spoke to my heart and that uplifted me more than anything. This morning I read from the book of Philippians. Funny how I'd forgotten all about God's command to "be anxious for nothing." I decided I'd better obey.

Mark grinned at the smiley face Ravyn drew. He felt encouraged. Highly encouraged.

Smiling, he tucked the card into his white jacket pocket and returned to the nursing station to tie up any loose ends before going home. All night long, new patients arrived in the ER, nurses had questions, and every so often one of his cronies spotted him, walked over, and started up a conversation. Most of his fellow residents, Mark had learned, were either pursuing a specialty here at Victory and/or had careers lined up at clinics or at other hospitals. Several of them were engaged and planned to get married this summer.

He squelched the pangs of envy. A family of his own appealed to Mark, although he knew it couldn't take precedence over the plans he already had in place. They began with a long overdue visit to New Hampshire where he'd spend some time with his family. After that, he'd start the candidating process, visiting two churches a week and gathering support for the mission field. By January of next year, Mark planned to join the team of medical personnel with whom he'd been corresponding via the Internet and occasional phone calls.

He sat down and drew in a deep breath. He needed to share his vision for his future with Ravyn soon, before she heard about it from someone else.

He patted the card in his pocket. Maybe now she was ready to hear about it.

Ravyn gave her reflection one last look and decided the kiwi green tank top and coordinating cardigan matched nicely with her navy capris. The dark blue slip-ons completed the outfit and gave her some height. Ravyn felt satisfied that she'd dressed appropriately for a casual dinner with Mark tonight. If she felt too warm, she could take off the lightweight sweater, and if the air conditioning in the riverfront restaurant had been cranked up, she wouldn't freeze.

We actually coordinated our schedules. She still couldn't believe it. Ravyn hadn't made time for a date in years; she usually opted to work an extra shift and make money. But, lately, she made time for the people in her life. She talked to Teala, her parents, and Violet nearly every day, relying less on her answering machine. Three times this week Mark had called, and Ravyn stopped whatever she'd been doing to converse with him. They'd turned out to be lengthy chats, too, but Ravyn enjoyed each minute.

And now their first official date.

She strode through the hallway of her posh condominium and paused at the kitchen table where she gathered her cell phone, sunglasses, and car keys. After slinging her small handbag's leather strap over her wrist, she continued out the door and into the underground parking area.

Today had been unseasonably hot in northeast Iowa for this last weekend in May.

Temperatures soared well into the nineties, but the air felt cool and dry in the basement area. Ravyn climbed into her car and started its engine, then drove out into the blinding sunshine. Before long, she began to perspire, so she closed the windows and turned on her vehicle's air conditioning.

As she drove through the hilly streets of Dubuque, Ravyn wished she had allowed Mark to pick her up like he'd offered. However, being the ever-independent woman, she chose to drive herself to the restaurant, but she'd forgotten it meant going through a rather seedy part of town. Seeing people on the sidewalks and street corners, laughing and carousing, Ravyn thought of how busy the ER would likely be tonight. The warm weather seemed to draw revelers from their homes and into the bars. Already she heard sirens in the distance.

Her cell phone rang and Ravyn worked the hands-free earpiece into place before answering the call.

"Hi, Rav," said Teala. "A few of us girls are going out for a pizza tonight. And guess who's coming? Carolyn Baker. You two haven't seen each other in eons. Want to come out with us?"

Ravyn couldn't help the smile. "Nope. I have a date."

Silence at the other end.

"Teala, I have never known you to be rendered speechless."

"Wow, we must have a really bad connection. I thought you just said you had a date."

Ravyn laughed, knowing her sister's facetious streak. "Oh, hush up. I'm going to dinner with Mark tonight. I guess it is an official date, but we're still just friends. I think."

"Your first date with Mark, huh?" Teala sighed. "I remember when Greg and I first started seeing each other — officially."

Ravyn had heard this story a hundred times, but she listened to it again. In fact, her younger sister talked for the rest of the drive to the steak house where Ravyn had agreed to meet Mark.

"Hey, Teala, I've got to disconnect. I'm at the restaurant now."

"Okay, *ciao.*"

Ravyn found a rare parking spot near the entrance and pulled alongside the curb. She unplugged her earpiece, then stuffed her cell phone into her leather handbag.

For a moment she sat behind the steering wheel and watched the many passersby. This was a bustling part of the city because of its close proximity to the Mississippi River and its subsequent recreational areas. The restaurant would probably be noisy and crowded, but oddly, Ravyn felt hardly intimidated. She was more looking forward to dining with Mark than worrying about getting shuffled about by pushy patrons.

An odd mix of anxious flutters and anticipation multiplied inside her. She bowed her head in a silent, quick prayer.

Lord, this thing with Mark — I think I'm a little scared. Losing my friend Shelley was tough; I can't imagine losing my heart. Will You please show me if this is a relationship worth pursuing?

Ravyn finished the petition to her heavenly Father before opening her eyes and glancing up — just in time to see Mark enter the restaurant with a tall, full-figured blond. Ravyn recognized the woman at once.

It was Carla, the x-ray tech from work!

TEN

Ravyn wrapped her palms around the steering wheel, wondering if she should take flight or fight. Mark wouldn't have been stupid enough to ask her out on the same night he asked Carla for a date — would he? But, perhaps, in all the busyness of finishing his residency, his schedule got mixed up.

No, it couldn't be.

Or could it?

Curiosity won over indignation as Ravyn climbed out of the car and stepped into the shadows of the historical red-brick building. She yanked open the rough-hewn door, using more force than necessary, and stomped inside the dimly lit establishment. She almost collided with Mark as her eyes adjusted from the sunlight.

Before even uttering a greeting, he cupped her upper arm and led her toward the restrooms. "Ravyn, I need your help." She felt his lips near her ear, drowning out the loud music. "On my way in, I met up with Carla. I don't know where she came from, but she's got a head laceration. I told her to wash up and then I'd look at it." Mark steered Ravyn toward the ladies' room. "Can you go in and check on her?"

She pulled out of his grasp. "Give me a break. Carla's an x-ray tech. She's more than capable of washing a gash on her head."

"ETOH."

That's all Mark had to say. Ravyn was well acquainted with the acronym. She arched her brows. "Carla's drunk?"

"Extremely."

Ravyn winced with embarrassment for overreacting. "All right. I'll check on her."

She entered the restroom, unable to ignore the relief zinging its way through her limbs, but stopped short when she saw the shapely x-ray tech sprawled out on the brown and beige tiled floor. Her back was up against the wall and her legs stretched out in front of her. Blood stained her long blond hair and the front of her two-sizes-too-small white T-shirt.

After setting down her purse near one of the three porcelain sinks, Ravyn knelt beside her coworker. "Hey, Carla? It's me. Ravyn.

Looks like you hurt yourself. What happened?" Ravyn carefully picked at strands of Carla's blond hair in order to get a look at the wound.

"I fell."

A knock sounded on the restroom door. Ravyn stood, crossed to the door, and opened it to find Mark standing there. He held out a pair of protective gloves.

"The bartender said he keeps a box of these handy. I s'pose that's not a bad idea in his line of work."

"Thanks." Ravyn sent Mark a grateful smile, took the proffered gloves, and let the door close. She pulled the protective coverings over her hands and returned to inspecting Carla's wound. Sorting through crusty strands of blond hair, she still couldn't see the woman's scalp. She stood and wetted some paper toweling and tried again.

On her knees next to her coworker, Ravyn did her best to clean the area. All the while she felt the other woman's stare.

Finally, she met Carla's gaze and momentarily scrutinized her features. Ravyn hadn't ever seen her up close before and never paid her much attention. She assumed they were peers, but now Ravyn realized that Carla couldn't be any older than twenty-one. Not any older than Teala.

"You hate me, don't you?" Carla muttered.

"I don't hate anyone."

Locating the laceration, Ravyn realized it required stitches. She straightened and crossed the room. She used another piece of paper toweling to pull on the door handle. Mark stood several feet away and she motioned to him.

"She's going to need some sutures and, considering her condition, maybe we ought to call an ambulance."

"Good as done." Mark pulled his cell phone from out of the pocket of khaki pants.

Once again, Ravyn let the door close and turned back to Carla, who continued her ramblings about how everyone from her boyfriend to her mother "hated her." After soaking more paper towels in cold water, Ravyn hunkered down and held the wad against her coworker's head. She watched as a tear slipped from the younger woman's left eye and drizzled down her sunburned cheek.

"Don't cry. It's okay."

A strange sense of pity engulfed Ravyn. She found it odd when usually she felt almost hard-hearted toward intoxicated individuals. She had observed a number of drunken souls at the low-income housing

134

units in which her family had lived. But this instance seemed different — perhaps because Carla was a coworker.

Ravyn recalled what she knew of Carla. She was never boisterous at work, like Liz, but kept mostly to herself. Her only fault, as far as Ravyn knew, was hanging out with a bunch of staff who enjoyed boozing at breakfast.

That, and lying about Mark, of course.

Carla began to sob, and while Ravyn suspected the show of emotion was alcohol-induced, she couldn't help feeling sorry for her.

"It's okay," Ravyn repeated. Her own sob session last week came to mind — one that couldn't even be blamed on alcohol consumption — and her empathy for Carla mounted. She, like so many people, needed help — needed to know God. Was this Carla's cry for help?

As if in reply, more tears cascaded down Carla's pink cheeks.

"Shh." Ravyn looped one arm around the younger woman's shoulders. "Everything's going to be all right."

"Maybe for you," Carla eked out. "You're dating a doctor who's not only great-looking and single, he's really nice, too." She choked back another sob. "My boyfriend can't seem to hold a job for more than two weeks. When he runs out of money it's suddenly *my* fault."

"Find another boyfriend." The answer seemed easy enough to Ravyn.

Carla tipped her head, giving Ravyn a curious stare. "In case you hadn't noticed, there aren't that many guys around to choose from these days. Half of them are married. The other half are divorced and come complete with court-ordered alimony payments. Either that or they have issues — like felony convictions."

"Where do you go to meet these guys? They sound like losers with a capital *L*." Ravyn shook her head. "Seriously, Carla, I think you're in need of a new hangout."

"Yeah? Like where? I suppose I could play Bingo on Friday nights at church with all the boring religious people."

Ravyn grinned. "Mark's religious. So am I. We're both born-again Christians."

Carla didn't look surprised, although she didn't have a comeback, either, but Ravyn let it go. She suspected her intoxicated coworker wouldn't remember much of what went on in here tonight; however, by God's grace, a seed could have been planted.

A seed . . . As the thought took shape, Ravyn felt suddenly privileged that God would use her to plant a seed of faith in another person's life. She didn't deserve to be an instrument of God's love; she could count on one hand all the times she'd attended church in the past year. Yet here she sat, on a cold, tiled floor with a hurting soul in her arms. Ravyn knew this event was no coincidence.

A hard knock sounded at the door, jarring Ravyn from her thoughts. She looked up to see Mark peer into the restroom. His dark gaze found Ravyn's. "Paramedics are here."

"Great. We're ready for them."

"Admit it," Mark said, grinning and pointing his fork at her. "When you walked into the restaurant, you were ready to chew me up and spit me out. I saw that gleam in your eyes."

"Gleam?" Ravyn batted her lashes in feigned innocence. "I have no idea what you're talking about." She sipped her diet cola.

"Whatever."

Ravyn tried not to laugh at Mark's skeptical expression.

After the ambulance arrived and transported Carla to the hospital, Ravyn had needed to change clothes. Since she had to return to her condo anyway, she'd suggested that she and Mark eat at the restaurant on the complex's lavish grounds. The temperature had cooled and it seemed a perfect evening to dine on the restaurant's patio, which overlooked the eighteenth hole.

"Do you play golf?" Mark asked, cutting his veal.

"I've played in the past, but that's not why I bought a condo here at The Pines, if that's what you're wondering." Ravyn watched the wind tousle his dark brown hair. "I think it's pretty out here. It's a gated community and each section of condos has a locked lobby, so I feel safe."

"That's important — to feel safe."

Ravyn agreed.

"I've often heard the safest place to be is in God's will, no matter where you're at here on earth, even if you live in the toughest of neighborhoods."

"Hmm." Ravyn gave it a moment's thought. "Yeah, I suppose that's true enough."

She thought back on her growing up years in the rundown public housing units. Her parents had left Ravyn and her sisters so vulnerable and unprotected around the riffraff they called neighbors. Anything could have happened to them. But, as Ravyn's father was fond of pointing out,

God had, indeed, protected them.

"I forgot. I have something for you." Mark stood and pulled what appeared to be a small envelope from the back pocket of his trousers. He reseated himself, then slid the paper item across the white wrought-iron table. "It's an invitation. My aunt feels compelled to have a party for me, although I've told her it isn't necessary." A look of embarrassment heightened the ruddy hue of his cheeks. It was a nice contrast, Ravyn thought, with the deep green polo shirt he wore.

"I don't blame your aunt for making a fuss. It's not every day that a person completes his residency."

"I know, but all the extra attention is embarrassing."

"You love it. Don't lie." Ravyn laughed at his hooded glance. Then, with the tip of her fingernail, she slit open the envelope and pulled out a three-dimensional, handmade card, inviting her to Mark's party.

"I wish I had Aunt Edy's time," he said. "She created about fifty of those cards."

"Impressive." Ravyn looked over the colorful invite before carefully placing it near her small purse. "And your great-aunt plays the piano, too?"

"Yep. And she bakes the best rhubarb pie

you ever tasted."

"She sounds like quite the talented lady."

"She is."

Ravyn noted the grateful expression on Mark's face as he forked some salad into his mouth. He chewed and swallowed. "Without my aunt and uncle's support, I would have never made it through my residency program. I owe them a lot."

As Ravyn listened, she picked at her grilled salmon.

"They believe in me and the goals I've set — goals that go beyond my medical training."

He sat forward in the candy-striped padded chair and set down his fork. "I never did tell you my plans for the future once I'm done with my residency."

"No, you never did. I'd love to hear about them."

As Mark began to divulge his passion for the souls in a tiny country off the Indonesian coast, Ravyn had a sinking feeling inside. She forced herself not to react negatively when she heard the words *medical missionary,* but it took so much effort she could barely concentrate on anything else he said.

"I'll spend my summer candidating at various churches," he added, reclaiming her attention. "Once I've accumulated enough support, I'll head overseas. The director of the missions team drew up a five-year contract, but he promised me furlough every eighteen months."

Was that supposed to make her feel better? It didn't. "So, in essence, all your time in medical school has been — a waste."

"A waste?" Mark sat back hard in his chair. "How can you say that? I'll soon be a board certified MD."

"Board certified in America." She shook her head, feeling disappointed in him. "And why would you ask churches to support you when you could earn a good living here in the U.S.? You could pay for your own missions trips overseas. I mean, think about it. You could make enough money here in the next couple of years to support yourself in a Third World country for a very long time."

Mark didn't reply and Ravyn suspected she had said too much. She stared down at her half-eaten dinner.

"There's accountability in enlisting churches' support for a group of missionaries," Mark stated at long last. "Not only will I have to answer to the Lord for my decisions and actions, but I'll report to a board of godly pastors."

Ravyn could see his point, but she still believed he was about to throw away all his years in med school if he followed through with this ludicrous plan. "Mark, in the five years that you'll be gone the health-care industry will have changed so much here in the United States that you might find yourself behind the times and unable to practice. Then what?"

"Then I —"

"Wait. Let me guess." Ravyn held up a hand. "You don't have a plan now, but you're going to *trust the Lord.*"

"Right. Minus the sarcasm, of course." He sent her a wry grin.

"Look, I believe that we, as Christians, must trust and obey God's Word and His leading, but I also think there's a fine line between blind trust and irresponsibility." She tipped her head, regarding him. "Your plan sounds like it teeters on the latter."

"Irresponsible?" Mark shook his head. "I disagree. What I've learned in med school is going to help me care for souls in a remote country who'd never receive health care if it weren't for me."

"And you have to do that full time for five years?"

"Well, yeah," he said, as if it were obvious. "It takes time to build a good testimony on a foreign mission field. The locals have to see that I'm genuinely concerned about them. Once they realize I can help them health-wise, they'll listen when I talk to them about their souls' eternal resting place."

He's a dreamer, Ravyn realized. She looked away and focused on a distant golf cart. Regret flooded her being. She had hoped to get to know Mark better. In fact, she had hoped to fall in love with him and live happily ever after.

And now who's the dreamer? Ravyn silently berated herself for her girlish fantasy.

"Many parts of the country are built up for tourism," Mark said on a persuasive note. "The capital city, for instance, has an urban feel to it. It's really a beautiful place."

"Where is this place again?"

Mark hailed the waiter and asked for an ink pen. Then he drew a rough map.

Ravyn felt her heart plummet to the depths of remorse. The small country was on the other side of the world.

"I visited there only once, but I immediately developed a burden for the island people."

"That's important." Ravyn forced herself to say something upbeat and encouraging. "They'll be lucky to have you there."

"I appreciate your saying so." Mark sent her a curious glance.

Ravyn didn't say any more. She already felt the pinch of guilt for her negative responses, but she battled her own emotions. Disappointment weighted her heart like lead. Next to Teala, Mark had become a confidant. She looked forward to seeing him at work. His sense of humor lifted her spirits. His easygoing outlook on life alleviated her day-to-day stress. His faith in Christ strengthened hers.

And now Ravyn found herself missing Mark already.

ELEVEN

"It's still early," Mark said, glancing at his wristwatch. "I'm sure we can find something fun to do."

"No." Under the moonlight, he watched as Ravyn shook her head. Several strands of her black hair fell against her face, and the humidity in the air kept them adhered to her pale cheek until she brushed them away. "I should go in."

Mark leaned against the white stucco archway that led to the complex's surface parking lot. He folded his arms across his chest. "Hmm, was it something I said — like I'm going to the mission field?" He couldn't keep the facetiousness out of his voice. He felt more than a little hurt at Ravyn's obvious rejection. Then, again, he had anticipated it.

She lifted her chin and squared her shoulders, and Mark fought off a grin. She might be petite, but her feisty spirit more than made up for her small stature.

"I'm very fond of you, Mark," she began, "maybe more than I should be, and I don't want either of us to get hurt." She raised a hand before he could refute her comment. "I can't just be your friend, either. The night you kissed me changed our relationship for me."

Mark lost his surefootedness as he bore responsibility for his actions. She was right: He had been the one to kiss her, and if it had impaired their friendship, there wasn't much he could do about it now.

"Our future goals are very different. Too different."

He hated where all this was leading, but supposed he should let her have her say.

"I hope to end up working in Madison at the University of Wisconsin Hospital. Overseas missions . . ." She shook her head. "Not for me. Besides, if that's what God wants, I can be a missionary on the job right here at home." A rueful grin tugged at her pink lips. "Maybe I'm more like my parents than I ever imagined."

Mark shifted his stance. "How so?"

"Mom and Dad chose the theater to try to reach people here in Dubuque. Just recently I've been able to see a mission field in my own backyard, too. I think of Jace, our GSW patient in the trauma room. Today's teens need to know there's Someone they can turn to with their anger and frustration. They need Christ. As weird as my upbringing was, I at least knew I had Jesus in my heart. Looking back, I can see how He was my source of strength and protection."

It did his heart good to hear her talk about the Lord. "I don't doubt there's a mission field here at home."

"And think of Carla, drunk and vulnerable in a public restroom," she pressed on. "I hate to even speculate about what might have happened to her if she hadn't stumbled into you — *literally*. There's an obvious a need in her life, too."

"You're probably right."

As her words sank in, Mark actually felt hopeful. What he heard Ravyn say was that she was *willing* to heed the Lord's voice when it came to serving others. Who could ask for more than that?

She glanced away. "The way things stand, Mark, there's really no point in us seeing each other."

"Hmm. Interesting. But what do you think God has to say about it?"

She swung her gaze back to his face and grinned. "You're very stubborn, aren't you?"

He pursed his lips in thought. "I like to think that I am determined."

"You say determined. I say stubborn —"

He laughed. The repartee wasn't lost on him. "But I'm not ready to call the whole thing off."

Still smiling, he leaned toward her, placing a kiss on her cheek. "G'night, Ravyn." He paused and stared into her dark eyes. She looked lovely under the glow of the moon. On impulse, he touched his lips to hers, stealing another quick kiss. "See you later," he whispered against her soft cheek.

Stepping back, he glimpsed her stunned expression and tried not to chuckle. But he grinned all the way through the parking lot and to his car.

With a long sigh, Ravyn entered her condo and dropped her belongings on the kitchen counter. *Determined, my foot. Mark Monroe is one of the most mule-headed men I've ever met.*

The phone rang and Ravyn searched for the cordless handset. She found it in the pillows on the sofa and pushed the TALK button. She half expected it to be Mark, so she felt surprised when her mother's voice wafted from the earpiece.

"You're not supposed to be home."

"Yeah, well, here I am."

"Teala said you were out with Mark tonight."

Ravyn swallowed the last of her annoyance. "I did go out with Mark, but I'm home early."

"Home?" Her mom paused. "Does your place feel like home? It's so odd not having you around here. I miss you."

Her mother's rare admission touched Ravyn's heart. On the other hand, independence is what Ravyn had wanted for years. "It's getting to feel like home. It'll take awhile to get the rooms furnished and decorated to my liking."

"I suppose that's true enough."

"Besides, I've always worked so much over the past years that I was never at home. You didn't miss me then."

"That's because I knew your bedroom was just upstairs, not on the other side of Dubuque."

Ravyn fought in vain to grasp her mother's logic. Finally, she gave up. "So, what's going on, Mom?"

"Oh, the reason I called — Dad and I wondered if you'd come to church with us tomorrow morning. Lunch afterwards. Our treat."

"Sure." Ravyn didn't have to think twice.

God wanted her time, and she could at least give Him a couple of hours a week.

"Would you like to ask Mark to join us?"

"No." Ravyn expelled a weary sigh. "You might as well know I told him I couldn't see him anymore."

Another pause. "Why on earth did you do that?"

Ravyn suddenly felt her temples begin to throb. "Mom, don't sound so panicked. There are other fish in the sea."

"Yes, but Mark is such a *nice* fish."

Ravyn smiled at the jest in spite of herself.

"What happened? Did you two have a spat?"

"No." Ravyn kicked off her shoes. "I can already tell that things between us aren't going to work out."

"What a shame."

"Yeah, it's a shame, all right."

Ravyn allowed her gaze to wander around the room, and suddenly the stark white walls seemed to have less potential. In fact, they looked more barren than ever.

In short, she thought, they resembled her heart.

"So, how'd the date go?"

Mark backtracked through the kitchen and spotted his uncle in the den. "Oh, just fine." He wasn't in the mood to divulge the details.

Uncle Chet seemed to read right through him. " 'Just fine'? That's it?"

Standing at the doorway, Mark nodded out a reply and looked at the TV screen. The NBA semifinals were on. "Who's winning?"

"Miami over Detroit." Uncle Chet lifted the remote and turned off the basketball game. "I'm not really into it." He lazed back on the plump sofa. "I want to hear about your date with Ravyn."

Mark gave him a shrug as he entered the room and sat down. "It started off with an intoxicated coworker at the steak house. She had a gash on her scalp, so we called an ambulance to take her to the hospital. But by the time the medics arrived, Ravyn needed to change clothes." Mark paused to explain. "Head lacerations can be messy."

Uncle Chet raised his hand, palm-side out. "Say no more. I get the picture."

"So Ravyn and I ended up leaving for another restaurant at the complex where she lives. Dinner was okay. We made it an early night."

"High drama at the steak house spoiled your romantic dinner, huh? That's too bad."

"No, actually, things went okay." Mark

stood. He still didn't feel ready to discuss the particulars, and he certainly didn't want his uncle to assume his "investment" wouldn't pay out. Mark planned to keep his end of the bargain. After all, getting him through med school and onto the mission field had been Uncle Chet's and Aunt Edy's dream all along.

Uncle Chet drew his bushy brows together, looking serious. "How does Ravyn feel about you living overseas doing missionary work?"

Mark marveled at the older man's perception. "She respects my decision." He didn't add that Ravyn didn't feel it was her calling. "We'll see what happens."

His uncle lifted the remote and pointed it at the TV. "Keep me posted."

"Sure."

Mark left the den and jogged up the steps and into his bedroom. He changed into a pair of baggy gym shorts and a comfy T-shirt. After washing up in the bathroom, he collapsed into bed and thanked God for the work He was doing in Ravyn's life — and his own, too. He also prayed for wisdom. On one hand, he felt obligated to respect Ravyn's wishes regarding their relationship. On the other hand, Mark wasn't willing to give up on her yet.

He closed his eyes and placed the future in God's hands, determined not to take it back. But first things first. He had a residency to finish.

TWELVE

The ER was abuzz with activity and Ravyn found herself in the thick of it. Three sick patients demanded her attention, two of them critically ill. It was all she could do to juggle their care. As usual, she did her best to ignore Mark's presence, although she found it difficult to have to ask him to sign off on orders. Over the course of the last several days, he'd done his best to act aloof and professional toward her, but every now and then forgot himself and behaved as though they were best buddies. More often than not, he caught himself, though, and was quick to apologize. However, he had Ravyn's emotions swinging like a pendulum.

And then there was Carla. She went out of her way to avoid Ravyn, but she took advantage of every opportunity to sidle up to Mark. At one point, Ravyn saw the two engaged in conversation and she told herself she didn't care. Mark could talk with whomever he pleased, and since it was most likely clarification on an x-ray order that Carla needed, he *had* to discuss it with her.

Ravyn berated herself for her childish notions. What's more, she despised the fact that she'd gotten sucked into the ER drama.

At last the time came for Ravyn to punch out, and she hurried to leave the hospital. Fatigue weighted her every limb, and she couldn't wait to get home and crawl into bed.

As she drove uphill toward the west side of town, she passed a fast-food place and her stomach grumbled. Ravyn realized she hadn't taken a lunch break and the last thing she'd eaten in the past twelve hours was a handful of pretzels from a bag that one of the unit clerks had opened. Pulling a U-turn, she maneuvered her car into the drive-through lane and ordered a breakfast sandwich and orange juice. Then she inched her vehicle toward the window, waiting her turn to pay for her food. She suddenly recalled how in their high school days she and Shelley would often hang out here with their other friends. Then one day she was gone. Vanished.

A rueful smile curved Ravyn's lips as she recalled how Shelley always talked about moving to California and becoming a famous actress. Perhaps she'd moved to the West Coast.

Ravyn completed her exchange with the cashier and drove off with her bagged breakfast. She continued to think about Shelley and, as she did, Mark's suggestion that she make peace with the past surfaced. Maybe it was time to look up Shelley and give her a call. In talking to her, perhaps Ravyn would be able to put all the hurt, and even betrayal, behind her once and for all.

At that moment, it occurred to Ravyn that Mark's reentrance into her life might have been for the sole purpose of settling matters with him. Could be God never intended for her to develop a romantic relationship with Mark.

But if that were true, then why did she feel so glum?

"My friend Jen Taylor gave me this phone number. Her sister-in-law keeps in touch with the Jenkinses."

Ravyn set down the cardboard box containing the last of her belongings here at her folks' house, and took the proffered slip of paper. "Thanks, Mom."

"Somewhere along the line I heard they moved to Florida. Jen said the Jenkinses still live there."

"I'll try this number and see where it leads me. Might be that God doesn't want me to find Shelley."

"Follow His lead, honey."

"I will."

Ravyn lowered herself onto one of the worn kitchen chairs and watched as her mom sipped her iced tea. She thought Mom resembled a stereotypical gypsy in her colorful, frilly skirt and white T-shirt. Her dark hair was pulled back and carelessly secured with a large silver barrette. Sterling hoops swung from her earlobes.

"It's a hot one today, isn't it? I don't recall the month of June ever being quite this warm and muggy."

"It's always hot and muggy in June. How 'bout we go to my place and swim in the pool for a while?"

"Sounds nice, but no can do. I have to be at the university in a half hour to sit in on auditions." Her mother leaned forward. "Think you'd like to try out for a part in your father's summer play? It's air-conditioned in the auditorium."

"I'll pass. Thanks."

"Is that sarcasm I detect in your voice?"

"Me? Sarcastic?" Ravyn grinned at her own quip while running her finger over the scarred kitchen tabletop. The thing looked like it had gone through both World Wars. In fact, most of the furnishings in her parents' home looked either battered or outdated, although, thanks to Violet and Teala, the house was clean and the furniture dusted.

Mom laughed and lifted her glass. The ice cubes tinkled. "Mmm," she said, sipping her brew. "Green tea on ice is fabulous. Are you sure you don't want a glass?"

Ravyn shook her head. "Thanks anyway. I have to get going." She sent her mother a teasing grin. "My air-conditioned condo awaits me."

"Oh, go ahead. Rub it in. Pool, central air . . ." Her mother gave a flick of her wrist. "La-dee-da."

Ravyn laughed and finger-combed her hair back off her perspiring forehead. "Maybe I'll have some iced tea after all." She stood, walked to the fridge, and helped herself.

"So what do you hear from Mark these days?"

"Not much. I see him at work once in a while, but that's it." Ravyn replaced the pitcher in the fridge and then, glass in hand, reclaimed her seat at the kitchen table. "The last thing he said to me was, 'Can I borrow your pen?' and I haven't seen him or my pen since."

The glib remark caused her mother to laugh, although Ravyn didn't add how difficult it was to see Mark when their shifts overlapped. The sight of him tugged on her heart in a painful way, and when their eyes met regret filled her soul. Mark was probably the only guy she'd ever met with whom she'd connected in some odd, supernatural way. He could read her as easily as the daily newspaper and, likewise, she sensed what went through his mind. Their so-called telepathy came in handy in the trauma room last week after a patient was brought in with life-threatening injuries from a motorcycle crash. She had guessed what Mark was going to say before he said it, and Ravyn knew their faith in Christ was, of course, the cornerstone of that mystical connection between them.

Still, she couldn't accept his plans for the future, but at the same time, she found herself feeling like she had when Shelley disappeared. A sense of loss crimped her heart. The truth was, losing two friends in one lifetime proved almost more than Ravyn could bear.

As she drove back to her condo later that afternoon, she heard the Lord's still small voice from within say, *I'll never leave you.* It brought tears to Ravyn's eyes and suddenly she felt immeasurably humbled. In spite of the fact that she'd neglected God all these years, He remained faithful and true to her.

Mark watched Ravyn flit around the ER like a little hummingbird. She seemed to filter out the nonessential chatter and concentrate on her work, which was commendable for the most part. But he overheard Liz say she was concerned about Ravyn burning out. Apparently, she'd been picking up extra shifts and she didn't take time out for lunch or her scheduled breaks. She assigned herself to the patients as they arrived instead of "sharing the wealth," as it were. Liz finally gave her a stern talking-to, saying, "What do you think this is? A one-nurse operation?"

And now, as Liz relayed the circumstances to a few of her friends, Mark felt saddened to hear it. In fact, he felt partially responsible. He suspected that Ravyn kept herself on the go so she didn't have to deal with her feelings for him. On the other hand, he could well imagine her calling him an egomaniac for assuming that he was the reason for her intense dedication to the ER. Perhaps it was wishful thinking on his part.

For all he knew, she had a lot of debt to pay off — and she had talked about purchasing a new car.

Mark stood and made his way toward the exit. He couldn't stand listening to the gossip, especially since Ravyn was the subject matter. However, if the worst they could say about her was that she worked too hard, she wouldn't be their topic of discussion for very long.

Strolling down the empty hallway, he considered any one of a hundred things he could do to occupy himself, but his thoughts always came back around to Ravyn. He wished he could give her a little moral support, but he was trying to give her some space. Besides, Liz would straighten her out. Then once he finished his residency he wouldn't be around to antagonize her with his mere presence.

The thought saddened Mark. He had hoped that by now Ravyn would have changed her mind and the two of them could at least be friends.

Talk about stubborn.

He paused by the glass doors that led out to the smoking deck. The rain poured down and lightning flashed in the distance. He recalled Ravyn mentioning her desire to do research at University of Wisconsin Hospital in Madison. She had lofty aspirations and they were every bit as important as his. She was all about her career. He was all about serving God overseas. Mark shook his head. They were hardly a match made in heaven.

Why, then, couldn't he just forget about her? *Lord, is it that You don't want me to forget about her?*

Over the last few weeks Mark had considered everything Ravyn had said when they'd had dinner together. Her remarks about medical school being wasted and him acting irresponsibly for gathering church support this summer were like scalpels slicing through to his soul. He began to wonder if she was right. After all, it was true that the health-care industry in the States would be far different when he returned from the mission field.

Are You refining my plans, Lord, to suit Your will, or is Ravyn a distraction?

The sound of rubber-soled athletic shoes squeaking against the polished floor signaled someone's rapid advance. Another staff member, he figured, due to the early hour. He straightened just as the object of his thoughts rounded the corner of the hallway, heading straight for him. He almost chuckled at the irony.

When Ravyn spotted him, her steps faltered. "Oh . . . hi." She hiked the strap of her vinyl lunch bag higher onto her shoulder in what Mark guessed was a nervous gesture. "I got banished from the ER for a half hour."

"Well, you don't want to sit on the smoking deck and eat your lunch. It's storming."

Ravyn swung her gaze to the window beside the doorway. Raindrops streamed down the glass pane. "Yeah, I guess it is."

Awkwardness hung between them like a thick velvet drape.

Mark turned to stare outside again. From the corner of his eye, he saw Ravyn pass behind him. He fought to hold his silence.

But he didn't win.

"Hey, wait."

She glanced over her shoulder.

"Can you spare a few minutes?"

"Sure." Ravyn pivoted to face him.

Mark stepped forward. "This isn't work related."

A little frown marred her dark brows. "Okay."

"Maybe it's sheer pride, I don't know. I haven't quite figured it out. All I know is I'm not handling getting dumped very well, not that it hasn't happened before. It has, but —"

"I didn't 'dump' you, Mark. I merely . . ."

She paused as if searching for the right words. "I just don't think anything between us is meant to be."

"Really? Then how come we're both miserable?"

Ravyn blinked and Mark realized the question erupted from some hidden place inside his being, surprising them both.

He sighed and figured it was too late to turn back now. He might as well bare the rest of his heart. "You never gave 'anything between us' a chance."

A look of remorse spilled over her features. Her matter-of-fact façade seemed to melt away before Mark's eyes.

"Listen, Ravyn, I'm not sure what God's will is for us, but why don't we take things one step at a time?" He pushed out a smile for her benefit.

She stood there looking like she might go into shock at any moment.

Mark decided a bit of levity wouldn't hurt. Placing a hand on her shoulder, he steered her toward the cafeteria. "But first things first: If you want someone to help you eat your lunch, I'm more than happy to oblige."

THIRTEEN

A moment of weakness. Mark had caught her in a moment of weakness. And now as she watched him devour her egg salad sandwich, Ravyn felt both amused and irritated. How could he have so easily finagled his way back into her life when she had fought so hard to shut him out?

Ravyn sipped her diet cola and decided she could, at least, act friendly. Friendly but distant. What would that hurt? Mark would soon be gone.

The thought nearly made her choke.

"I haven't had egg salad in years."

She felt oddly pleased that he enjoyed it. She'd whipped it up early this afternoon.

"So what's new with you?" he asked. "We haven't talked in about three weeks."

Ravyn chose not to remind him that it was on purpose they hadn't talked, other than business, of course.

"Not too much." As she regarded him,

Ravyn decided Mark reminded her of her dad in many ways. They both were hard-working and strong-minded, possessed a good sense of humor, and had a cavalier outlook on life.

The latter trait, unfortunately, was a source of all kinds of problems, and Ravyn knew that to be true firsthand.

"You've been working a lot of shifts, huh?"

"Yes, but I did manage to find some time to play Sherlock Holmes."

"Oh?" Mark arched a brow, looking interested.

"I tracked down Shelley. I found out she's living in Chicago. She's got a talent agent and everything. She must be a successful actress."

"No kidding?"

"Yep. She goes by the name of Jeanne Shelley now. Those are her first and middle names reversed. Anyway, her agent said he'd get in touch with her and have her call me. That was two days ago." Ravyn peeled open the foil top of a yogurt carton while Mark snooped through the rest of her thermal lunch bag. He found her bag of potato chips.

"Mind if I eat these?"

"Go ahead. I eat enough junk in the ER. Somebody always has food to share."

"I think it's that way on just about every

floor." Mark tore open the bag. "But I have yet to find fruit and vegetables getting passed among the staff."

"That's because fruits and veggies are healthy." Ravyn laughed. "True comfort food is high calories, fat, and sugar."

"Thanks for the clarification." Mark grinned and tossed a few chips into his mouth. "So . . . back to Shelley. Do you think she'll call you?"

"No clue." Ravyn took a bite of yogurt and marveled at the peace she felt inside. "I've prayed about it and I'm leaving the matter up to God. I made the attempt and that's all I can do."

"You're a wise woman."

"It's elementary, my dear Watson."

Mark winced at her poorly feigned British accent.

"Sorry. Guess I'll leave the acting to Shelley."

He nodded, grinning all the while. "Good thinking."

Ravyn laughed. "And speaking of acting, my dad held auditions last week. His production of *Soul's Agony* will run from late August to Labor Day."

"Wish I had some time. I'd participate. Sounds like fun."

"My dad wrote the script himself, which

is a first, and according to my mother, it's brilliant."

"Your parents are incredible people."

"I agree. They are." Ravyn finished her yogurt, then reached into her lunch bag and retrieved a sandwich bag filled with store-bought chocolate cookies.

Mark began helping himself. "It takes time and dedication to write and direct a play — might even be more work than being a doctor or nurse."

"I know where you're heading and you can stop right there." Ravyn took a bite of one of the sugary rounds. "I know my folks work hard. I never said they didn't. I just believe that there are times when God expects Christians to make use of what He's given us — like an able body and an intelligent mind — to earn a decent living."

"So where does that leave missionaries? Don't you think they earn a decent living?"

"I don't know. I'm sure some do — if they're practical."

"Practicality has nothing to do with it. Let's use Jesus as an example. He said birds had their nests, but the Son of Man didn't even have a place to lay His head. Jesus didn't have a job. He trusted God for everything, including His next meal."

"True. But He was also a carpenter before

168

that, indicating He did, in fact, have a skill and hold down a job."

"I think that's kind of a stretch, Ravyn." Mark sounded a bit amused before turning serious once again. "Let's never forget He gave up everything including His life to preach the gospel. His disciples gave up their livelihoods as fishermen to follow Him. Likewise we're to do to the same."

"Yes, but on the other hand, we never read anywhere in the Bible that Luke gave up being a physician even though he wrote one of the Gospels."

Mark couldn't seem to find a comeback. Either that, or he gave up the argument altogether and all too easily.

Ravyn glanced at her wristwatch and realized a half hour had passed. She packed up her lunch bag. "Look, I don't have a problem supporting missionaries," she said at last, "as long as they're willing to support themselves if need be."

They stood and made their way out of the coffee shop.

"Kind of hard to find employment when you're in a foreign country."

"I'm not referring to foreign countries. I was thinking of my parents when I said that. My dad went months without earning a dime when, instead, he could have found a job and might have been a witness to his coworkers."

Mark listened without reply and Ravyn felt a check in her heart. She knew she wasn't much of a witness for Christ on the job. Was that what Mark thought, too?

They walked partway down the hall in silence before Ravyn spoke again.

"My dad used to say that if you work in the world, you get worldly. But, for myself, I don't see a way around it."

"I think it's all about one's personal, individual, and divine calling." Mark stuck his hands in the pockets of the long white coat that residents and MDs were required to wear over their scrubs. "Missionaries and Christians in full-time ministry highly respect those on the front line, working in the world." He chuckled. "They're the ones who support us."

"Good point." Ravyn couldn't find fault in that logic. "I guess I never thought of it that way."

She paused outside the women's locker room and held up her bag, indicating she wanted to stop and put it away.

"Thanks for the sandwich."

"You're welcome."

Mark gave her a charming smile. "Catch you later. I'll try to call you this week.

Maybe we can find some time to get to-gether."

"Okay. That'd be nice."

Ravyn entered the locker room and re-alized what she'd just agreed to. She smacked her palm against her forehead. *Oh, that man! He messes up my thinking!*

Mark found his uncle sitting on a lawn chair in the backyard and walked outside to join him. "How are you feeling this afternoon?"

"Pretty good." Uncle Chet gazed at him and smiled.

Mark pulled up a white plastic chair and sat down beside him.

"I'm watching the weeds grow since your aunt won't let me pull 'em." Uncle Chet gave a disgruntled snort, but the wet stain covering the front of his striped T-shirt indicated that, indeed, he had been garden-ing.

"You're not supposed to be exerting yourself. Your heart is still on the mend. At least Aunt Edy is following the cardiologist's orders."

"Bah!" Uncle Chet waved one hand at him. "I'm just fine. Besides, working in the garden is just as much work as walking — it's less of a bore, too."

Mark shook his head in disappointment.

"I hope you're behaving. I'd like to have you around for a while."

"This subject is hereby closed — says me."

"Okay." Mark knew better than to argue with his obstinate uncle.

"So you're off work for a while now, huh?"

"Couple of days."

"Won't be long now and you'll be a full-fledged doctor."

"Yeah, and maybe then you'll listen to me when I tell you to take it easy."

Uncle Chet shook his finger at him. "Knock it off."

"All right."

Mark chuckled and glanced around the vibrant green yard. A month or so ago his aunt had planted the vegetable garden that Uncle Chet had been tilling when he suffered his heart attack. Already leafy plants sprouted from the dark, rich soil.

"So how's your little blackbird these days?"

"Ravyn?" Mark grinned at his uncle's silly nickname for her. "Funny you should mention her. I'm planning to drop in and see her."

"Never drop in on a woman, Mark. That's a dangerous thing to do."

He took a moment to consider his uncle's advice and recalled the last time he'd dropped in on Ravyn. She had seemed embarrassed about her less than perfect appearance, but Mark thought she'd looked fine. So she wasn't all dolled up. It had mattered little to him. On the other hand, if it was a big deal to her, then maybe he should call first.

"You serious about this young woman?"

Again, Mark digested the question. "Not sure yet," he answered in all honesty. "I've been focused on finishing my residency. First things first, I guess."

"You're not planning to be around this summer," Uncle Chet pointed out. "That's why I asked."

A wave of reality crashed over Mark. What was he thinking? He could hardly court Ravyn by cell phone — and that's assuming she agreed to be courted. So far he'd cajoled his way into her life.

He sat back in his chair and put his feet up on the adjoining plastic chair. Remorse permeated his being. Who was he kidding? He had no right to drop in on Ravyn today.

FOURTEEN

Ravyn nibbled the inside of her lower lip as she waited for Mark to finish his conversation with another MD. Her conversation with Shelley weighed heavily on her mind, and with her parents in the throes of a new play and Teala absorbed in her romance, Ravyn decided Mark would make an efficient sounding board. He was, after all, the only other person who knew of the situation.

"Mark, can I talk to you?" She hailed him as he turned and started down the hallway.

He wheeled around at her question. "Ravyn." He smiled and walked back toward her. "I didn't see you standing there."

"I guess my scrubs sort of blend in with the wallpaper." She grinned at her jest. "Do you have a little time?"

He glanced at his watch. "A little. What's up?"

She sensed he was busy in spite of his willing reply. "It's kind of involved. I can try to catch you at a better time."

He paused but then his features relaxed. "No, this is fine. The ER's quiet. No guarantee it'll stay that way."

Ravyn agreed and she lowered her voice in case another staff member happened to be close by.

"I talked to Shelley. I had to call her agent back and this time he gave me her number."

"And?" Mark folded his arms.

"Well, I think she might be in some sort of trouble. She sounded . . ." Ravyn searched for the right word. "I don't know — desperate. In a hurry. Like she didn't want to be overheard and there was a lot of noise in the background. She repeated her address about three times and practically begged me to visit as soon as I could. We had no time for chitchat. She said she had to go and hung up. That was it."

"Ravyn, if you're asking for my advice, I'd say stay out of it. If Shelley is in Chicago and in trouble, then it's probably way over your head to help her. Big city. Big trouble."

He spoke Ravyn's exact thoughts, but the niggling inside wouldn't abate. "I sort of feel like I should go."

"Then don't go alone." Mark checked his watch again. "Listen, I have to fly. Talk to you later."

He dashed off, leaving Ravyn to wonder at his aloofness. She realized they were at work and it wasn't the time or place to convey emotional sentiments, but that had never hindered Mark in the past. Besides, his response seemed rather harsh for a prospective missionary.

With her thoughts in a whir, she returned to the emergency room's arena area. She picked up her work right where she'd left off. In the early morning hours of the night shift, it was typically quiet, except on weekends when the bars emptied out. Ravyn much preferred a steady twelve hours to sitting around doing mindless paper shuffling.

Several feet away, a few nurses, the staff physician, and a security guard gabbed to pass the time. They talked shop and Ravyn's interest was piqued by a particular case they discussed.

Liz met her gaze. "Hey, don't just stand there and eavesdrop, pull up a chair and join us."

Ravyn smiled. By now she'd grown accustomed to Liz's boisterous antics. In fact, the day Liz called in sick, the ER didn't seem the same without her.

Unable to resist the invitation, Ravyn stepped around the parameters of the

nurses' station and began conversing with her coworkers.

About an hour later, a patient with abdominal pain admitted herself to the ER. The chat group disbanded. At a physician's request, Ravyn hurried down the inner corridor in search of a piece of equipment. She passed unused exam rooms and a tiny break area where a coffeepot was kept along with a refrigerator and microwave oven. As she glanced in that direction, Ravyn did a double take and slowed her pace. She saw Mark and Carla sitting at the small round table, having, what appeared to Ravyn, an intimate conversation. Mark was leaning toward Carla, talking in such a hushed tone that Ravyn couldn't hear what was being said. Carla looked mesmerized.

Ravyn clenched her jaw. Now what was this all about? He'd acted curt to Ravyn — why? So he could rendezvous with Carla?

She chided herself for thinking the worst, but then it occurred to her that she never wholly trusted Mark because she never could quite believe that Shelley had lied so many years ago.

As she stood in the hall, memories came rushing back — Shelley's incessant prattle about how madly in love she was with Mark and then her tears when he broke her heart.

As great an actress as Shelley might have been then or may be today, Ravyn didn't think anyone could feign such pain and despair.

So did that mean Mark was a philanderer with an incredible façade or had Shelley been a misguided teenager?

As Ravyn spied his ongoing discussion with Carla, she couldn't help but suspect he wasn't as upstanding and genuine as he appeared. Maybe there was something to his nickname "George" after all.

Disappointment rocked her soul. The Daniels and the Gideons of the Bible just didn't exist in this day and age.

Carla cleared her throat and Ravyn snapped to attention. Mark turned in his chair.

Ravyn avoided his gaze. "Dr. Thomas is looking for the portable ultrasound machine." She forced a sturdy tone. "Have either of you seen it?"

Both shook their heads and when Ravyn glimpsed Mark's expression, she noted he didn't even have the good grace to look guilty.

That's the stuff creeps are made of, she thought, turning on her heels and walking away. Continuing her search, she finally located the machine and wheeled it to the patient's room where she absorbed herself in her work. Mark's residency couldn't end fast enough as far as Ravyn was concerned.

But now she was more determined than ever to visit Shelley and hear the truth from her former friend's lips. Once and for all.

"You know she's jealous, don't you?"

Mark looked away from the now empty doorway where Ravyn had stood moments ago and regarded the smirk on Carla's face.

"Ravyn's a Christian, too," he explained. "Believers feel the same emotions everyone else does. But we have something more to help us overcome the destructive ones, like envy and jealousy. We have our faith in Christ."

"So what's your point?" Carla sat back in her chair.

"My point is, Ravyn will get over whatever is eating at her. And if you have questions in the future about what we discussed here, I hope you'll ask her."

"Why would I do that? She hates me."

Mark shook his head. "No, she doesn't. Ravyn was genuinely concerned about you the night you fell and hit your head."

Carla's blush surfaced through her sun-tanned cheeks. "Must you keep bringing that up?"

"Carla, from what you've told me, it sounds like you're teetering on a very slippery slope. Your behavior is going to get you hurt — or killed."

"I don't have a drinking problem, all right?" She folded her arms. "I just . . . like to have a good time. What girl doesn't?" A provocative smile curved her full lips. "And if you weren't so religious —"

"Time for me to go." Mark stood. "Just remember, everything I told you is in the Bible. You can look it up for yourself and you can ask Ravyn. She might seem like a tough cookie," he added with a grin, "but she's all marshmallow inside."

"For your sake, I hope that's true." Carla laughed.

Mark silently agreed as he made his way to the front of the ER. Ravyn hadn't exactly looked pleased, not that he took any pleasure in the fact she was jealous. However, it did affirm what he felt in his heart: he and Ravyn had strong feelings for each other.

Unfortunately, they were miles apart in their ideals and philosophies. Ravyn had pointed out that fact from the beginning.

Mark decided God had a lot of work to do and, humanly, it seemed impossible. In a matter of days, Mark would leave for the rest of the summer with only short stops at his great-aunt and uncle's place through the fall. He would, of course, see them during the Christmas holiday. Then come January, he'd be gone for what might as well be forever where he and Ravyn were concerned.

And by the looks of it, she wasn't speaking to him — at least not verbally. But the angry sparks shooting from her eyes might rival the upcoming Fourth of July fireworks.

Mark leaned against the counter near the unit clerk's desk where Ravyn wrote in a patient's chart.

"It's not what you think, okay?" he ventured.

"Okay."

Yeah. That was way too easy, Mark thought with a facetious bent.

He blew out a sigh but chose not to press the issue. Not here. Not now. He'd let Ravyn cool off awhile. He wanted to leave Dubuque knowing that at least the two of them were on good terms.

After that, it was all up to the Lord.

Ravyn packed her car, then slid behind the steering wheel and began her weekend trip to Chicago. According to the map she'd printed off the Internet, the drive would take about four hours.

181

Turning onto U.S. 20, she sped across the High Bridge, also known as the Julien Dubuque Bridge. It was a steel, arched structure that spanned the Mississippi River and connected the state of Iowa with Illinois. As she continued on toward the interstate, Ravyn marveled at how quickly she'd been able to make arrangements for this trip. She'd swapped a few shifts with two other RNs, and since everything came together so smoothly, Ravyn knew it just had to be God's will that she visit Shelley. She felt the Lord's leading in this. She rejected the inner nudging that she'd planned this trek in order to spite Mark and, regardless of his warning, she was going alone. She convinced herself, and not for the first time, that she didn't care what he said, did, or who he talked to.

No, what mattered now was that finally, after a decade, Ravyn would finally learn the *real* truth.

FIFTEEN

After checking into a hotel and dropping off her belongings in her room, Ravyn climbed back into her car. She'd asked for directions to Shelley's place, and the clerk behind the front desk had warned her that she was heading into a rough part of the city. Tapping her fingers against the steering wheel now, Ravyn wondered if she should go. Obviously, Shelley wasn't as successful as Ravyn imagined.

But she's in trouble and I want answers. Ravyn decided that, in a sense, she and Shelley needed each other.

Her resolve gelled, and Ravyn stuck her key in the ignition. Within a half hour, she was maneuvering her car through downtown Chicago. Twice she turned right instead of left, but finally she found Shelley's address.

She stared through her window at the dirty, brown brick building that contained an establishment called The Sunset Grill on its lower level. Ravyn assumed Shelley's apartment was upstairs.

She got out of her car before she lost her nerve. Loud music blared from a car stereo somewhere down the street, and several feet away two shaggy-haired men in muscle shirts hovered beneath the hood of an automobile that had obviously seen better days.

Ravyn scurried to the brown wooden door at one end of the building and rang the doorbell. The smell of deep-fried food lingered in the air. She prayed for God's protection and tried not to second-guess her decision. Feeling nervous at no answer, she knocked on the door.

A waitress came out of the diner, wearing a grubby striped apron over a white tank top and red shorts. She was reed thin, and her dyed reddish blond hair was pulled back into a ponytail, exposing an inch or so of her natural light brown roots. Her hazel eyes sparkled with question — and then recognition set in.

"Ravyn!"

She blinked, fighting the shock. "Shelley?"

"Oh, thank God you came. I didn't think you would." Shelley stepped forward and wrapped her bony arms around Ravyn. She smelled of grease and cigarette smoke, and

Ravyn almost choked.

She politely pulled back and stared up into her former friend's gaunt face. Words failed her. Shelley was a mere shadow of the healthy, vibrant friend Ravyn remembered. This woman looked twice her age.

"My son told me someone was at the door."

"Son?"

Shelley nodded. "I'll introduce you." She removed her apron. "Let me tell Flint I'm leaving."

"Flint?" Ravyn felt like an echo, but she could barely think straight. Was Shelley ill? Was she dying? She didn't look well.

"Flint owns this dive. Now, wait right here. Don't leave, okay? I'll be right back."

Against her better judgment, Ravyn complied. Moments later, Shelley returned, expletives following in her wake. Ravyn didn't think she'd ever heard such blue language.

"Ignore him. Flint's a creep. He'd have me working twenty-four hours a day if he could."

Shelley unlocked the adjacent door, then took Ravyn's elbow and steered her inside. The air in the tall stairwell that led to the second floor felt hot against Ravyn's skin, and that prevailing smell of grease seemed to ooze from the faded green walls.

When they reached the top of the steps, Shelley unlocked another door and bid Ravyn entry. Although tidy, the sparse living room had a dingy feel to it and smelled of stale cigarette smoke.

"Flint lets me rent this furnished apartment. He supposedly takes the money out of my paychecks, but in six months of working for him, I haven't seen a cent and when I asked about it . . ." She shook her head. "Let's just say things got ugly. So I'm living off the tips I earn and, believe me, that's not a lot."

"But you have an agent, so I thought —"

"He gets me gigs doing exotic dancing at nightclubs. He's a lousy agent."

Ravyn didn't know what to say.

"But I quit dancing years ago. I'm really trying to clean up my act, pardon the pun."

A husky little boy suddenly barreled into the room but stopped short at seeing Ravyn.

"Marky, this is the friend I told you about."

"Is she going to help us?"

"I haven't asked her yet." Shelley's tone held an incredulous note. "Give us a chance to get reacquainted, will you?"

The kid shrugged at the reprimand and eyed Ravyn. However, her mind hadn't gone much further than the child's name. *Marky?* Tension began throbbing at her temples as she took in his nut brown hair and chocolate-colored eyes. His face looked flushed and Ravyn thought the temperature in the apartment had to be nearing one hundred degrees.

"He looks like his dad," Shelley said, sounding chagrined.

Ravyn felt sick.

"Marky's ten. You can do the math and figure it out." Shelley waved a hand at her son. "Go in my room and watch TV so me and Ravyn can talk in private."

The boy wrinkled his face at the request, but he obeyed.

"I was pregnant when I left Dubuque."

Ravyn turned on her. "Why didn't you tell me?"

"Because you're so good, Ravyn. Whenever I watch *Gone with the Wind* I think of you. You're like Melanie, always looking out for everyone else —"

"Oh, please." Ravyn rolled her eyes. "There's no similarity. Trust me."

"But that's how I've always seen you, Rav. And, to the contrary, I'm a Scarlet O'Hara. I knew what I did was wrong, but I loved Mark so much that I gave in to what I wanted instead of doing what was right."

She had the good grace to look ashamed of herself. "I've continued that pattern ever since, I'm afraid."

Ravyn's stomach churned.

Shelley expelled a weary breath. "When my parents found out I was pregnant, they sent me away to live with my dad's cousin in Florida. Mom and Dad were embarrassed and told all their church friends that I had some weird flu. That's why you took over my role in the play, remember?"

She nodded. How could she forget?

"I hated it at Aunt Petunia's house. That was her name. I'm not kidding. *Petunia.* But, unlike the flower, she wasn't pretty. She was a mean old biddy who arranged my son's adoption and never once asked me how I felt about it. So, before Marky was born, I ran away with a guy I'd met. He had some friends in Arkansas, so that's where we went. Then, after Marky entered the world, Pete dumped me and things have spiraled downhill from there." Shelley's laugh had a bitter edge to it. "As bad as it sounds, it got worse."

"I–I'm sorry to hear that." Ravyn struggled to process the information.

"I didn't dare go back to Dubuque. I figured everyone I knew hated me. Besides, by that time my parents had moved to

Florida to be near Aunt Petunia, who was ailing with something or another. I forget."

"People in Dubuque would have understood and forgiven — even helped you. My family would have taken you in."

"Not according to my mother. She lived in constant fear her neighbors and church friends would discover she had an illegitimate grandson, and she had me believing I could never go back." Shelley's lips formed a grim line. "Incidentally, my parents disowned me a long time ago."

She motioned for Ravyn to sit down on the couch and then called for Marky to bring them each a can of diet cola and a glass filled with ice.

"I've been battling a, um, drug problem," Shelley further admitted. "But I've stayed clean now for over three months. It would have been longer, but Flint . . ." She shook her head. "Never mind. Let's just say he's not exactly a good example for me."

"He gives you drugs?" Ravyn felt outraged and appalled, although she'd heard similar stories in the ER and even before she'd started working at Victory.

Shelley nodded in answer to her question. "But a couple of guys from the rescue mission come into the diner almost every day. They've been encouraging me."

Marky reentered the living room, balancing the items his mother requested on a round serving tray.

"Want me to pour?" he asked, looking eager.

"No. Get back in my room — and don't try to listen in on our conversation, either."

The boy frowned at his mom before stomping off.

"Thanks, Marky!" Ravyn called to his retreating form.

"He's a good kid," Shelley said. "Takes care of me."

Ravyn found herself empathizing with the boy. After all, she'd taken care of her parents.

"I take it Mark doesn't know he has a son."

"Oh, he knows." Shelley took a long drink of her cola. "That's one of the first things I did is slap a paternity suit on him. He's supposed to send a check every month, but he doesn't have any money."

Ravyn tried to swallow the bile rising in her throat. "He knows? But . . . that can't be."

"It's true. Why are you so surprised? He's always been a womanizing jerk."

Disbelief showered over Ravyn. *Mark knows?*

A long minute passed in silence, then Shelley spoke again. "Look, I need some help. I've got to get out of here and I can't go to the mission. Not with Marky. Trust me, it's no place for a kid."

Ravyn blinked and tried to push aside her shock long enough to listen.

"All the friends I've made are — well, the wrong kind of friends, if you know what I mean. I just want to leave Chicago forever. I need to find a real-paying job and get Marky in a good school before he — he ends up like me."

"What do you want me to do?"

"Get me out of here, Ravyn. Please." Shelley leaned forward. "When you called last week I began to think there really is a God in heaven." She twirled the sweating glass in her palms. "I would have stayed on the phone with you longer, but Flint said if I did, he'd deduct the time out of my pay — which I still have yet to see. He just finds more ways to get me further indebted to him."

She wetted her lips. "Ravyn, let's get in your car right now and go — somewhere. Anywhere. Drop me off in a town that looks even remotely promising."

"And then what? Do you have any money saved?"

Shelley shook her head and lowered her gaze. A second later, she looked back at Ravyn. "But I'm sure I can find a job soon enough."

"At a sleazy nightclub or another greasy spoon?" Ravyn thought she might be naïve, but she didn't consider herself totally ignorant. "That won't help you. You'll end up falling back into your old lifestyle."

"Oh, but, please. I can't stay here." Shelley stared at her with wide and pleading eyes.

Ravyn pursed her lips, thinking about lending Shelley money. But, again, that posed a danger because Shelley could always use the borrowed funds to buy drugs.

"Okay, let's think over the situation. We need a plan." Ravyn had more or less spoken her thoughts and didn't expect a reply.

But Shelley set one hand on her shoulder and gave it a little squeeze. "Ravyn, it's Friday. It's a hot summer afternoon and there are going to be parties up and down this street tonight. Some friends might stop over with beer and drugs and I'm afraid that I might —"

"Okay, I understand." Ravyn sensed Shelley's hope was gone and her will was fading fast. "Then there's only one thing left for us to do."

"That is?"

"You and Marky are coming back to the hotel with me until we can figure out a practical solution."

Relief washed over Shelley's sunken features. "Thank you. It's at least a step forward." She sagged against Ravyn. "You're a true godsend."

"Hey, watch this one!"

Ravyn turned just in time to see Marky jump off the diving board. His backside hit the water, creating a huge splash that reached both her and Shelley as they sat perched on the edge of the hotel's outdoor swimming pool.

"I'll have to nickname him Tsunami," Shelley joked.

Ravyn had to laugh in spite of all the drama earlier this afternoon.

After helping Shelley and Marky gather and pack their meager articles of clothing and miscellaneous items, they stopped at a discount store where Ravyn purchased some necessities for them. She had also bought swimsuits, thinking the pool would be a fun activity for Marky, and she'd been right: he now behaved very much like a typical ten-year-old boy.

It hadn't taken long before Ravyn realized

she liked Marky. In fact, she liked him a whole lot more than she liked his father at the moment; however, she'd already noticed problematic behavior. Shelley had good cause for concern. Her son knew some colorful language and used it when he didn't get his way. He also tried to steal a portable CD player at the store, but Shelley caught him before they reached the cash register and made him put it back.

And Mark could have been a positive influence in his son's life. How can he think about helping people in a Third World country when he doesn't even care about his own child?

Deep in Ravyn's soul she sensed something wasn't right, but she wrote it off as being in a state of shock and even denial. She immediately recalled Mark sitting with Carla alone in the break room and his nickname George in the ER. Maybe all the rumors were true after all.

What a scammer.

Ravyn felt heartsick. It seemed her suspicions about him had been right. Worse, he'd played her for a fool and she'd fallen for his practiced charm. Then again, that's what she'd come to Chicago for: to learn the truth about both him and Shelley.

"I feel like I'm on a luxury vacation," Shelley said as she made swirls in the pool with her bony foot. "Marky and me — we're indebted to you big time."

Out of sheer politeness and nothing more, Ravyn pushed out a smile. The sight of Shelley in a bathing suit was worrisome. She looked rail thin. Her collarbone jutted out from beneath her onion-paper thin skin, and her ribs were visible with each deep breath Shelley took. Her knobby joints were equally as prominent and her flamingo bird legs didn't look strong enough to even support her.

Ravyn glanced back at Marky. It was obvious to her that both mother and son had enormous issues to tackle. She felt overwhelmed, and not for the first time this afternoon. What would she do with these two? Shelley needed counseling — Marky did, too. They needed money and a safe place to live, and now Ravyn felt responsible for their wellbeing. On the other hand, if she wasn't careful these two might suck her time dry and deplete her savings account.

Lord, I've gotten myself into a real mess.

Just then Ravyn remembered Jace, the teen in the trauma room with the gunshot wound. She recalled her desire to help save his life and, later, her wish to help other teens before they found themselves in dangerous situations. On the path Marky treaded, he was headed for disaster. At least Shelley had the wisdom to see that fact before it was too late.

Ravyn drew in a deep breath and steadied her emotions. With God's help, she could think up a course of action.

"Okay, here I go again. Watch this one!"

Ravyn looked toward the diving board. Marky did another cannonball into the water, and she and Shelley couldn't help but laugh once more.

Mark glanced at his watch. Three o'clock. He gazed around his aunt and uncle's yard where people stood mingling. He'd hoped to catch a glimpse of Ravyn, but it didn't look like she would show. Then again, what had he expected? He never did have another opportunity to talk to her since the shift she'd found him discussing the Lord with Carla and probably jumped to erroneous conclusions. Now his residency was completed, so he couldn't count on seeing Ravyn at the hospital again. He'd tried to call her all weekend, both at her condo and on her cell phone, but Ravyn never answered.

Oh, she was miffed at him, all right.

Or had she gone to Chicago by herself to try to find Shelley?

Mark wondered if he was right on both accounts. He had stopped by Ravyn's folks' house yesterday and no one had a clue as to her whereabouts, not even Teala. He knew from their lengthy discussions in the past that Ravyn was close to her younger sister. Why had she taken off, leaving the state, without telling someone about her plans? That was downright dangerous. If her intent had been to worry Mark sick, it worked, although he'd been careful not to upset her family with his questions and suspicions.

But what if something had happened to her?

The thought kept intruding on Mark's thoughts, and he didn't think he'd ever forgive himself if Ravyn was hurt — or worse.

At that moment, a couple of friends paused to congratulate Mark on "surviving" his residency.

"You made it, dude!" Andy Carey declared.

The two men balled their fists and knocked knuckles.

Mark chuckled and forced himself to relax and forget about Ravyn. She was, after all, an adult who could think for herself and make her own decisions.

Besides, Mark didn't know if he was even

remotely welcome in her life in the first place.

SIXTEEN

In the dark and quiet hotel room, Ravyn lay awake, thinking. She'd spent two and a half days with Shelley and Marky. She'd listened with a patient ear as Shelley told her one woeful tale after another. Her life thus far had been marred by one bad decision after another. Shelley claimed she was now more than ready to start anew.

The only question was where.

Ravyn ignored the answer that came to her time and time again. The last thing she wanted to do was take Shelley and Marky back to Dubuque and let them live with her. However, God's Holy Spirit seemed to prompt her to do exactly that.

But I don't want to support them. What if they steal from me? Where are they going to sleep? I don't want to give up my new bedroom set to Shelley. I worked hard for the things I have.

"Mom?"

Marky's whispered voice stilled Ravyn's thoughts.

"Mom, are you awake?"

"Shh." Shelley hushed him. Both she and Marky shared the queen-sized bed next to Ravyn's. Shelley said it was a far sight better than anything they'd slept on in years. "Be quiet or you'll wake up Ravyn."

"Mom, I don't think she wants to help us." Marky tried to speak in undertones, but it was like a foghorn trying to sound like a flute. Ravyn overheard him with little trouble, and the comment irritated her all the more. She'd been nothing but cordial and generous. She'd spent hundreds of dollars on them between buying new clothing and paying for all their meals. What else did the kid expect?

"Go to sleep, Marky."

"But, Mom, if Ravyn doesn't help us what are we going to do?"

"Will you quit worrying and go to sleep already?"

The silence that followed pressed in on Ravyn. She knew how Marky felt. As a little girl she had lost plenty of nights' sleep, fretting over what would become of her family.

"Walk by faith, Ravyn," her dad used to say. But it sounded so irresponsible to her young ears. She now knew the concept was one of God's commands. However, as a child, Ravyn wanted to find comfort in knowing her parents were in control and that they'd take care of her. In short, she longed for a sense of security.

And that's what Marky was asking for from his mother — security — except Shelley couldn't offer any. She battled her own demons and needed caring for herself.

Ravyn's heart softened. *Okay, Lord. For the first time in my life I'm going to walk by faith and take Shelley and Marky home with me. All I ask is that You help me each step of the way.*

"Okay, time for a meeting." Ravyn scooted upright in her bed, then reached over and flipped on the lamp.

Shelley and Marky squinted at her from the next bed.

"I've got a plan — and one that I honestly believe is God's will."

Marky bolted into a sitting position while Shelley propped herself up on one arm.

"Are you going to help us, Ravyn?" he asked. His dark eyes shone with anticipation.

"Marky, I've been helping you all weekend."

"Yeah, I know, but —"

"And we're very grateful," Shelley cut in

201

before reaching backward and rapping her son in the shoulder.

He frowned and rubbed his arm.

"But I know what you're asking for, Marky, and I think I have the answer."

"What is it?" He appeared hopeful once more.

"You and your mom," Ravyn said, peering at Shelley, "are coming back to Dubuque with me and you're going to stay with me in my condo."

Shelley sat up a little straighter. "Back to Dubuque?"

"You'll have support there. My parents will help. No one is going to judge you. It's not as if you're the first single mother in the world — even though your folks forced that lie down your throat."

"I know, but —"

"And, Marky, where I live there's a pool and a golf course —"

Ravyn didn't even finish her sentence before the kid let out a whoop of happiness.

"Are you sure, Ravyn?" Tears glistened in Shelley's eyes.

"I'm sure but, um, there is one problem." The Dariens came to Ravyn's mind. They were so proud of Mark. Did they know he had a son?

She stood and pulled on her bathrobe.

"Shelley, let's go out on the porch and talk so Marky can sleep and dream of doing super-sized cannonballs in the pool at his *new home*."

"Yes!" He flopped onto his pillow. "But now I'm too excited to sleep. Can I watch TV?"

"No. It's late." Shelley turned out the light.

Ravyn crossed the room, pushed back the thick drape, and slid open the patio door. Shelley followed her outside. They stood on the small veranda that overlooked the hotel's parking lot.

"Thank you, Ravyn." Shelley enfolded her in a hug. "Thank you. I don't know what we would have done —"

"You're welcome." She stepped back. "I feel God wants me to help you out and I want to — trust and obey."

Shelley nodded, still looking grateful. "So what's the problem? I'll do anything you want. I'm trying to quit smoking. I'll sleep on the floor —"

"It has nothing to do with you." Ravyn drew in a deep breath, hoping for both tact and boldness. "It's, well, Mark has relatives in Dubuque. They're sweet people and, while I couldn't care less if Mark's reputation is soiled, hypocrite that he is, I don't

203

want to hurt his aunt and uncle." She paused. "Do you think they know about Marky?"

"Mark has an aunt and uncle in Dubuque? I didn't know that. He's from out of state."

"Yes, but he's been living with his aunt and uncle — actually his great-aunt and uncle — while he finishes med school and his residency."

"Med school?" Shelley shook her head as if to clear it. "Wait a second — are you talking med school as in *Mark is a doctor?*"

"Yep, but unfortunately for you and Marky, he's bound for the mission field, so he still doesn't have any money." Ravyn tipped her head, thinking over the situation. "Unless he's lying about the mission field, too."

"Who's lying?"

"Mark." Ravyn stood arms akimbo and her anger mounted. "Oooh, that rat! I'll bet the whole medical missionary thing was a bunch of bunk so he could get out of paying child support."

Shelley gaped at her. "Mark is a *doctor?* No way!"

"Yes, 'way.' I met him in the ER when I started my job at Victory Medical Center. He just finished his residency." Ravyn thought back on the week. "His last day in the ER was Friday, and after he passes his boards, Mark will be a bona fide MD."

"Ravyn . . ." Shelley appeared confused. "I've done a lot of mind-altering drugs. I admit that to my shame. But I'm sober enough and sane enough to know that" — she shook her head again — "there is no way on God's green earth that Mark Leland is a medical doctor. No way."

"Who?" Ravyn felt her rage abate, only to be replaced by confusion. "Mark *Leland?* Who's that?"

"Marky's dad." Shelley regarded her askance. "Who are you talking about?"

"Mark Monroe."

Shelley scrunched up her face. "Who's that?"

Ravyn felt her throat go dry and humiliation flooded her being. "I thought *he* was Marky's biological father."

"Monroe?" Shelley shook her head. "Never heard of him."

"Yes you have."

The banter suddenly seemed comedic and Ravyn burst into a laugh, although nothing about the misunderstanding was funny. It had caused her much anguish this weekend, and it might have devastated Mark's plans for his ministry. But at the moment, Ravyn couldn't control the chortles bubbling up from somewhere deep inside her being.

Standing beside her, clad in the gray sweatpants and red tank shirt that Ravyn had purchased two days ago, Shelley regarded her with a frown. "Were you drinking at suppertime?"

"I don't drink." Ravyn tried in vain to suppress her ill-timed humor. "I'm sorry. I think I'm just so relieved."

"I feel like I just entered the Twilight Zone." Shelley combed her fingers through her shoulder-length hair, then set her hands on her bony hips.

Ravyn collected her wits. "Okay, let's start over. Who is Marky's father?"

"Mark Thomas Leland, formerly of Rochester, Minnesota, and currently a resident of St. Cloud. He flunked out of college and does odd jobs, but he's unemployed more than he works. Who are you talking about?"

"Mark Monroe. He was your leading man in my dad's summer production eleven years ago." Ravyn's mirth was replaced by a deep-seated sorrow. She'd believed the worst of him at every turn.

"Oh, yeah — him. I remember now. He was crazy about you, Rav. Remember how I said we were both going to end up with a guy named Mark?"

"Sure, I remember. But I thought you said that to imply I was getting in the way of your romance — *with Mark*." She tipped her head to one side and eyed Shelley. "Who is Mark Leland? Where did you meet him? When did you meet him?"

"That same summer — during the production. He was the light guy. He'd been going to school in Dubuque, taking summer remedial classes. Your dad somehow met him and convinced him to volunteer to work the spotlights for the play."

Ravyn searched her memory and came up empty. "I have no recollection of him."

"He wasn't a Christian."

She shrugged out a reply. She didn't know him.

"I talked about him all summer."

"I thought you meant Mark *Monroe.*"

"Oh." Shelley halted and seemed to consider her answer. "Well, that's understandable. I was sneaking around with Mark Leland. I didn't want anyone to know. But you were my best friend. I couldn't help telling you about him."

"Right. And I always felt responsible for — for whatever made you leave Dubuque. Until two days ago, I never knew you were pregnant and your parents sent you away. I thought Mark Monroe broke your heart and you blamed me because . . ." She recalled the last scene of the play and Mark's kisses.

"Monroe was more interested in you than me."

Ravyn nodded and pulled her bathrobe tighter around her. The night was warm and humid, but with so many emotions pummeling her, she felt exposed and vulnerable.

"So you thought Marky was Monroe's kid? And what? Have you two rekindled that little spark from the past?"

"Sort of." Ravyn stared down at her bare feet.

"Hmm. I'm surprised you've been so nice to us all weekend. If our roles were reversed, I think I'd want to punch you in the nose."

"Thanks, *friend,*" Ravyn quipped.

"Yeah, I'm horrible, all right." Shelley sounded serious as she gazed over the parking lot. At last she turned back to Ravyn. "But see how good you are? You've always been that way — always ready to help someone in need. I wasn't surprised when you told me you're a nurse."

She felt another jab in her conscience and looked up. "You're wrong, Shelley. I've been anything but good where Mark's concerned. I even went so far as to question his integrity and his character. He never once lost his patience with me. Instead, he told me he

208

cares about me and he's phoned me at least four times this weekend. I've ignored his calls. I actually thought I — I hated him because I believed the worst-case scenario."

"There's a very fine line between love and hate, isn't there?"

Ravyn shrugged. With so many emotions bombarding her at the moment, she couldn't begin to identify her true feelings for Mark.

"Don't be so hard on yourself. Why wouldn't you believe the worst? You just admitted you can't recall meeting Mark Leland and it's not like I introduced you two or anything. I was off in my own little world, doing what I wanted to do. I gave no thought for anyone else."

"So every time you mentioned Mark, you meant Leland and I thought Monroe?"

"Sounds like it."

Ravyn tossed a glance at the stars that dotted the heavens. "Unbelievable."

Shelley folded her skinny arms and leaned against the wrought-iron rail of the porch. Next, Ravyn saw a silly grin curve her lips. "Wow. So, after all these years, you met up with *your* Mark again, huh?"

"Yes, but he's leaving the day after tomorrow, and we're at odds."

"Too bad." Remorse and wistfulness clotted Shelley's voice. "A good man is hard to find."

After having breakfast with a few friends, Mark returned to his great-aunt and uncle's house and began cleaning his bedroom. He sorted through his dresser drawers and closet. The chore didn't take long since Mark hadn't been home much during the last eight years. In fact, he hadn't experienced much of life outside the hospital, classroom, and, occasionally, church since he started med school and, after that, his residency program. Mark hoped he'd adjust to reality.

He moved to the large walnut-finished desk and emptied one drawer after another. Term papers, spiral-bound notebooks, admission letters, billing statements, handwritten comments and suggestions from professors — all were both useless and priceless mementos as he strove to achieve his goals. Mark could hardly believe that day had arrived.

His cell phone rang and he rushed to answer it but then reminded himself he wasn't on call anymore. He didn't have to jump. With a glance at the number on the external display, he felt more than a little surprised.

He flipped open his phone. "Ravyn. I didn't expect to hear from you *so soon*." He cleared his throat after the pointed remark. He'd only been trying to reach her for three days.

"Very funny."

Mark grinned, stood, then stretched out on his bed while he talked. "So what's up?"

"This is going to take awhile."

He glanced at his wristwatch out of habit more than anything else. "I've got some time. What's on your mind?"

"Well, first I want to apologize for not showing up at your party Sunday afternoon. I was in Chicago. I found Shelley."

"I figured. But I also know you weren't happy with me last week —"

"Yeah, I'm sorry about that, too. I guess I was puzzled when you were short with me in the hallway and then —"

"I had the neuro team hassling me about that patient we had in the ER, the one with the neck injury. As for Carla," he added, guessing her thought process, "I was witnessing to her, Ravyn."

"I'm not surprised."

Mark went from feeling defensive to defused by her agreeable reply. He'd fully expected her to challenge him. "Are you okay?"

"Yes. It's just been a rough weekend."

He listened as Ravyn began telling him about her friend Shelley, how she was in the throes of overcoming a drug habit, how she had a ten-year-old son — named Marky.

His gut lurched as possible allegations flitted across his mind. But an instant later, Ravyn quelled his mounting concerns. Shelley kept in touch with the boy's father, whose name just happened to be Mark.

Ravyn went on to explain how Shelley met the guy. "Do you remember him?"

"Vaguely."

"Well, that's more than I remember of him."

Mark pieced the circumstances together. On one hand, he could see how the case of mistaken identity occurred. On the other, he felt the sting of injustice and it wounded him to realize that Ravyn had struggled to believe him these last two months.

"I couldn't leave Shelley and Marky in that sweltering dump of an apartment. It was worse than any of the low-income units I lived in as a child. So I brought them back with me. Shelley really wants a chance at a new life, except — we already had an argument over cigarettes. I told her I wouldn't pay for them and Shelley's going crazy. She wants to smoke so badly that she's snapping at Marky and me. It's all I can do to keep my patience."

"There are over-the-counter remedies that might help Shelley."

"I know. I plan to pick something up for her when we go to the store this afternoon. She's making a grocery list right now. That's why I thought it'd be a good time for me to sneak out onto the deck and call you." A moment's pause. "Believe it or not, I didn't phone you to discuss Shelley and Marky."

"Oh?" He stared at the familiar white ceiling and wondered at the reason for her call. Did she need a favor?

Mark's pride cried out for retribution. *Hang up on her! Whatever she asks, refuse!*

However, the better part of him knew that if it were within his power, he'd help her any way he could. He cared about her and nothing she said or did would change the fact.

"What did you want to discuss?"

"Actually. I need to tell you something." Another pause. "I want you to know how truly sorry I am for — well, for jumping to conclusions and thinking the worst about you right from the start. I was so wrong."

The apology quieted his nagging indignation.

"I've done some soul-searching these past

three days and God showed me that I've been selfish, angry, skeptical, bitter, and, well, maybe even jealous."

He grinned. *Maybe?*

"I hope you can forgive me."

His grin became a smile. How could he *not* forgive her? The Lord wouldn't allow it, and neither would his heart.

"All's forgiven."

He heard her expel a sigh. "Good. I know you leave tomorrow and —"

"Hey, how 'bout if I bring over a movie and a couple of pizzas?" Suddenly Mark didn't feel ready to wrap things up and say good-bye to Ravyn. He sensed their relationship could take a turn for the better, and he hated to miss an opportunity to see her again before he left Iowa. The fact she admitted to "maybe" feeling jealous encouraged him in a weird sort of way. "Do you feel like some extra company?"

"Sure. I could use some Christian reinforcement. And Marky will be happy with pizza. The kid eats nonstop."

"Good. Then it's a plan. I'll be over about six."

The conversation ended and in one swift move, Mark sat up and bounced off the bed. Pocketing his cell phone, he walked downstairs and informed his great-aunt that he wouldn't be home for dinner. Then, with renewed enthusiasm, he finished cleaning out his desk drawers.

SEVENTEEN

Sitting cross-legged on her sofa, Ravyn sent up a quick prayer while Mark explained the way of eternal salvation to Marky. After viewing a Christian movie about a boy with cancer who had one last wish to learn how to bull ride, Marky was full of questions. Even though Ravyn knew her walk with the Lord wasn't what it ought to be, she'd experienced the reality of her faith time and time again, and she prayed Marky would come to know Jesus in a personal way, too.

"God loved all of us so much that He sent His Son, Jesus Christ, from heaven to save us." Mark sat on the floor as he spoke. He appeared relaxed in his tan cargo pants and striped vintage-style cotton shirt, which he wore untucked; however, Ravyn sensed his zealousness. "Just like the character in the movie pointed out, we've all done things that are wrong and that's why we need the Lord."

"I thought *Jesus Christ* was a swear word," Marky admitted.

"Well, it's a sin to take God's name in vain," Mark explained. "People take God's name in vain when they use Jesus Christ as a swear word. But if we're talking about Him and how He's the One who saves us, then it's okay to say His name."

"Oh." Guilt reddened the boy's face before he looked over at his mom as if for confirmation.

"It's true." Shelley dabbed her eyes, wet, in part, from the movie's sad ending. "I should have told you about the Lord a long time ago, Marky, but I was —" She barely eked out the rest of her sentence. "I was living a life far away from God."

Marky appeared both uncomfortable and confused. He turned to Ravyn. "Can I have another piece of pizza?"

"Sure." She gave him a smile. "Help yourself."

He shot up from where he'd been sitting on the floor, grabbed his paper plate off the coffee table, and dashed into the kitchen.

"This is all foreign to Marky," Shelley said. "I don't think he's ever been to church in his entire life. And don't say it." She held her hand up, palm-side out. "I know it's my duty as his mother to teach him about God, but I haven't exactly been on my job and I take responsibility for it."

Mark stood. "I wasn't about to condemn you, and I doubt Ravyn would, either."

"She'd have good reason." Shelley stared at the tissue box in her lap. "You both would."

"Don't start in on yourself again." Ravyn reached across the length of the sofa and touched Shelley's shoulder. "You took a wrong turn in life, but you're headed in the right direction again."

"I agree." Mark stretched. "It's good you're willing to take responsibility for your actions."

Marky reentered the room. "Hey, can I see what else is on TV?" He picked up the remote with one hand and took a bite of his pizza with the other. A juicy piece of sausage tumbled onto the light-colored carpet. It bounced, leaving two blotches of greasy tomato sauce on Ravyn's expensive area rug.

"Oh, now look what you did," Shelley said. "Where's your plate?"

"I didn't think I needed it," Marky replied with his mouth stuffed.

Ravyn swallowed down her sudden impatience and steered the ten-year-old back into the kitchen. *This isn't the kid's first spill,* she reminded herself as she grabbed a handful of paper towels and pulled out the spray bottle of carpet cleaner from under the sink, *and it won't be the last.*

Without a word, she scrubbed out the spots before they became stains. Meanwhile, Shelley asked Mark various medical questions.

"I want to quit smoking for good, but I don't want to get fat. I heard people gain a lot of weight when they give up cigarettes."

Ravyn pressed her lips together and congratulated herself on her restraint. It was on the tip of her tongue to tell Shelley that she could use a few pounds on that bony body of hers.

Lord, I'm feeling bitter-spirited. Take it away and give me Your peace.

She reentered the kitchen and tossed the paper towels into the garbage.

"Sorry, Ravyn." Marky stared at her with wide, repentant brown eyes.

Her heart softened. "It's okay. It's just a rug." She tousled his dark hair. "When you're done eating, wash your hands, and then you can watch TV, okay?"

He nodded before taking another bite. His expression said all was right in his world again.

Ravyn realized, and not for the first time, that he was basically a nice boy. He just needed love and discipline — and lots of patience.

She stooped to put away the carpet solution and saw that Mark had followed her into the kitchen.

"It's after eight thirty. I need to get going. My plane leaves early tomorrow morning."

Ravyn stood slowly to her feet. She was surprised at the swell of disappointment mounting inside her. She pushed out a smile. "I'm glad you came over. Thanks for bringing the pizzas with you."

"You're very welcome." He inclined his head toward the door. "How about if you walk me out?"

She had secretly hoped he'd ask. "Sure, but let me get something first." She traipsed to her bedroom and made her way to the dresser, where she lifted a small gift-wrapped box from its polished surface. While out grocery shopping this afternoon, she'd managed to stop at the mall and pick up a congratulatory present for Mark. It wasn't especially unique or expensive, but she hoped he'd like it.

She carried it in one hand discreetly at her side as she backtracked down the hallway.

"Keep the DVD," she overheard Mark say. "Watch it as much as you want to."

Marky shrugged a reply, seeming more interested in his cold pizza.

Meanwhile, Shelley climbed off the sofa and gave Mark a hug. "I wish you all the best."

"Thanks — and I'll be praying for you."

"Good. I need it."

Ravyn headed to the door, opened it, then she and Mark walked in silence to the elevator. Ravyn pressed the button to call the car to her floor.

"I've got to hand it to you," Mark said at last. "You're a brave woman to take on a Goliath of a project such as Shelley and her son."

"I'm not brave. I'm scared to death."

The elevator doors opened and they stepped inside.

"Could have fooled me."

Ravyn didn't reply but watched the illuminated numbers above the doors go from 3 to 1. When they reached the main floor, the elevator stopped and the doors opened.

"My advice, not that you've asked for it or anything . . ."

Ravyn grinned.

"Keep your eyes on Christ and you'll be fine. Remember Peter when he wanted to walk on water like the Lord? Jesus said,

'C'mon.' So he did. But the moment Peter doubted, he began to sink into the sea. Jesus had to pull him to safety."

Ravyn listened as they strode through the bright lobby. She remembered the biblical account.

"I think sometimes when God allows us to do great things for His glory, we start doubting and sink before accomplishing the mission."

She cast a glance his way. "Do you ever doubt your calling?"

"More times than I'd care to admit."

Ravyn suddenly regretted all the negative remarks she'd made. She certainly wasn't an encouragement to him.

"As for your situation, it looks like things have fallen into place. You have a plan, and Shelley seems both willing to go along with it and grateful for the help."

"Yes, she does."

Ravyn herself had much to be thankful for, particularly after her dad came up with "the plan" to which Mark referred. As of tomorrow morning, Shelley began her new secretarial position under the direction of Joan Drethers, the pastor's wife. Joan ran the office at the church Ravyn's parents attended and she needed assistance. She'd also earned a degree in biblical counseling years ago, so the setup seemed perfect. Meanwhile, Ravyn would continue her third-shift position in the ER and look after Marky during the day until school started in the fall. When Shelley came home in the afternoon, Ravyn would sleep and then Shelley would be home at night with her son.

Ravyn only prayed she could occupy a ten-year-old boy for eight hours a day.

They neared the lobby's front entrance and Ravyn touched Mark's arm. "Can you spare just a few more minutes?"

"Sure. In fact, I had hoped I'd get a little time alone with you."

Ravyn wondered at the remark while pointing to a corner where two printed-upholstered sofas and several coordinating armchairs had been placed near the impressive floor-to-ceiling stone hearth. The lobby in each section of this large condominium complex resembled an expansive great room which all occupants could enjoy. Tonight, however, the place was empty except for an occasional passerby.

Ravyn and Mark sat down on one of the couches.

"I bought you something."

"You didn't —"

"I know I didn't *have* to." She smiled at

his look of embarrassment. "I wanted to."

"Well, thanks."

Ravyn scooted sideways and tucked her leg beneath her as she watched him open the gift. A smile curved his lips when he saw the gold-faced watch with its black leather band.

"I realize you might have a bazillion watches. I know I do. But this one is sort of special." Ravyn pointed out the smaller face within the large one. "It's like two watches in one, and now wherever you go and whatever time zone you're in, you'll always know what time it is in Dubuque, Iowa."

"Thank you, Ravyn." Mark leaned over and planted a quick kiss on her cheek. "I'll think of you when I wear it."

Now it was her turn at embarrassment, although it was short-lived. Torrents of remorse followed. How could she have misjudged him so completely?

"Mark, I'm sorry."

"For what?"

"I feel like I've wasted the last two months when, in truth, I could have enjoyed your friendship."

"If I hadn't ruined it by kissing you."

"Well, yeah." Ravyn fought off a smile and Mark sent her an amused grin. "But I've changed my mind about that — about our friendship."

"Oh?" Mark arched a brow.

Before she could explain, an elderly gentleman sat down in one of the nearby armchairs and opened the newspaper. With their privacy interrupted, Mark took Ravyn's hand and stood, pulling her up from the couch with him. He nodded toward the door and she followed him out of the lobby and into the sultry June air. To the west, the horizon was aflame with the last of the sunset as they strolled through the guest parking lot.

"Now, as you were saying — you changed your mind?"

"Yes. It had to do with something Shelley said over the weekend. After hearing about her disastrous relationships, I came to the conclusion that any healthy, meaningful relationship develops from a friendship first."

"I agree."

"And, of course, the Lord has to be its foundation."

"That goes without saying."

They reached his car and Mark unlocked the door. He placed the gift Ravyn had given him inside and then turned back to her.

"I'm sorry I nipped our — friendship in

the bud. But maybe it's for the best since you're —"

"Headed for the mission field," he finished for her.

"I was going to say *leaving*."

"Really?"

"Yes."

He gave a quick bob of his head, then lowered his gaze. When he looked up again, his gaze held a spark of mischief. He dipped a brow. "Of course there is the fact ye thought I was a black-hearted scoundrel."

Ravyn laughed at his antics.

"In that case, ye had good cause to sever our friendship," he continued.

She applauded. "Good pirate imitation, Monroe. My dad would be proud."

He took a bow.

Again the feelings of regret; they might have had fun together if she'd only given him the benefit of the doubt.

"Are you ever coming back?" The question rolled off Ravyn's tongue before she could stop it.

"Yeah, I'll be back." Mark stepped forward and gathered her into his arms. "Around Christmastime."

Ravyn wrapped her arms around his midsection. December seemed like a million years away.

"Will you wait for me?" His lips brushed against her temple and then he stepped back. "I'd like a chance to continue this conversation."

Looking up into his dark eyes, she barely got the chance to nod before Mark folded her into another embrace and pressed a fervent kiss against her mouth. Ravyn's senses took flight. Suddenly she felt sixteen again.

And then the moment ended.

"I'll call you."

Ravyn fought her disappointment.

"You have my cell phone number."

She nodded. "Take care of yourself." Her throat felt tight with unshed emotion.

He sent her a smile before climbing behind the wheel of his car. She walked away, unable to watch him go. She made her way to the lobby and, once inside, she strode to the elevators.

As she rode the car to her third-floor condo, Ravyn made a startling self-discovery: She'd fallen in love with Mark Monroe. Perhaps she'd loved him all along.

But now . . . was it too late?

EIGHTEEN

Ravyn walked down the maroon-carpeted aisle of one of the smaller theaters on the University of Dubuque campus. Her father's production would be held here this year, as were all rehearsals. From his vantage point, Dad saw her coming and waved.

"Okay, everyone!" he called to his cast. "Let's all take a fifteen-minute break!"

The people onstage set down their scripts and began conversing with each other.

Ravyn reached the front of the auditorium and hugged her dad.

"Hi. How's Marky been behaving?"

"Good. Your mother and I kept him busy." He chuckled. "Between helping us out and his baseball practice each morning, I'd say we're successfully taking the wind out of the boy's sails." Dad's gaze brightened. "It's smooth sailing from here on in."

Ravyn agreed. "I'll take him home now and let him go swimming and that should *anchor his ship in the harbor,*" she teased, "at least for today."

Her father's jolly laughter rang throughout the empty theater. He slung his arm around her shoulders and gave her an affectionate squeeze. Then he planted a juicy smooch on the side of her head.

"Dad, please." She grinned and pushed him away.

He laughed again. As annoying as his shows of affection could be at times, Ravyn truly enjoyed them. What's more, she appreciated her parents' help these last two weeks with Marky. In ten short days, he'd morphed into a child again.

Shelley, on the other hand, seemed to struggle hour by hour, day by day. Sometimes Ravyn felt exhausted just getting Shelley to the church office where she worked six hours each day. As sad as it seemed, her friend hadn't worked an honest job in all her life. Rousing herself out of bed, showering, and getting dressed on time for her job each morning involved self-discipline, which was all new to Shelley. Even so, Shelley only had to recall the horror of her existence in Chicago, and all complaints were quelled.

Ravyn rounded up Marky, then said her good-byes to her mom and dad before leaving the redbrick building. Together she and Marky traipsed to the curb and climbed into Ravyn's car.

"Did you have fun this afternoon?"

"Yep. I was painting."

"I see that." Ravyn smiled as she noted the dried green and blue paint on his knuckles and under his fingernails. "A good swim in a chlorinated pool should fix that."

"Fix what?" He gave her a curious glance.

"The paint on your hands."

Marky seemed to notice it for the first time. "Oh, guess I didn't wash good enough."

Ravyn laughed. Typical boy.

They arrived home and changed into their swimwear. Ravyn grabbed a couple of towels and her cell phone. Minutes later, they were playing volleyball in the pool. Other children who lived in the condominium complex had seen them splashing and laughing and decided to join in on the fun. Soon the pool was filled with squealing kids.

Ravyn decided to take refuge in a deck chair on the sea-green tiled deck where other parents sat observing the ruckus. In conversing with her neighbors, she became better acquainted with them, and she realized what terrific social icebreakers kids could be.

Shelley had arrived home from work and showed up at the poolside in her denim skirt and T-shirt.

"I had a hunch this is where I'd find you." She pulled over a deck chair and sat beside Ravyn.

"You're home early."

"Joan had a dentist appointment, so she dropped me off."

"Oh, okay." Ravyn pointed at Marky. "Look at him over there. He's having a ball."

"So I see."

Shelley watched her son for several long minutes. Unidentified emotions played across her thin face before she turned in her chair and faced Ravyn. "I felt like quitting today. I got my first paycheck and the amount is laughable. I used to make better money in one night at the dance club than a whole week at the church office."

Ravyn grimaced. "You didn't quit, did you?"

"No. But I was going to. Except, now that I see Marky . . ." Shelley expelled an audible sigh. "I feel like God is showing me I'm doing the right thing. I won't get rich or famous, but I can do what's best for my kid. At this rate, he might actually grow up to be a decent human being."

Ravyn's heart went out to her friend. She reached over and set her hand on Shelley's arm. "Be assured. You're doing the right thing. You don't have to worry about money right now. You're my guest. Indefinitely. Maybe we should go to the bank and open a savings and checking account for you so if you need something —"

"I was hoping we could do that."

"But not cigarettes."

Shelley sent her a dark glance. "All right. No cigarettes."

"Cigars are off limits, too," she teased.

Shelley laughed. "I don't smoke cigars, you nut."

Ravyn grinned.

The next few minutes passed in silence as they watched the kids swim. Ravyn felt encouraged that Shelley mentioned the Lord showing her something and influencing her decision to stay at her job. It was progress.

"Did you hear from Mark today?"

Ravyn wagged her head. "Not yet."

"But you will. I noticed he's called every day since he left."

"Yes, he has. I keep thinking we'll run out of things to talk about, but we never do."

"If I were you, I'd hang on to that guy."

Ravyn reclined in her chair. "I'm trying to

figure out how to do that."

"What you do you mean?"

"Well, as much as I love and respect my parents, I don't want to live the way they did, always relying on other people to support them financially. You remember how it was. And now I happen to fall for a guy who's going to be a missionary."

"Just for the record, I think you had it better at home than I ever did." Shelley crossed one slim leg over the other. "Your family was always laughing and having fun, but my folks were serious and worrying all the time about what the neighbors thought."

"I mean *financially*. Sometimes we didn't know where our next meal was coming from."

Shelley paused as if to digest the remark. "I don't recall you guys ever being in dire straits. Besides, missing a meal here and there never killed anyone. It's not like you, Teala, and Violet were starving to death."

"Shelley!" Ravyn couldn't believe her friend's lack of empathy.

"One time I went on a binge and I don't think Marky ate for days. He was just a little guy, too. I'm so ashamed." After a glance at her son in the pool, Shelley turned back to Ravyn.

"And your point is?"

"I guess what I'm saying is that your parents are human. Sure, they probably made plenty of mistakes. But they're good people who help others all the time, and you — well, you're the same way. Look at how you're helping me out. I cringe to think what could have happened to Marky and me if you hadn't stepped out of your comfort zone and come to Chicago."

Ravyn didn't know whether to bristle at the reprimand or feel flattered by Shelley's gratefulness.

She laughed in spite of herself. Then she rapped Shelley on the knee and stood. "Come on. Let's try to get to the bank before it closes."

"So, what do you hear from George lately?"

Ravyn glanced up from a patient's chart to see Liz standing beside her with a teasing gleam in her eyes.

"We miss him around here. The new residents aren't nearly half as much fun to tease."

"I'll tell him that. I'm sure Mark will be flattered." Ravyn laughed.

"Seriously, what's he doing?"

"Right now he's at a large church in Wisconsin, helping with Vacation Bible School." Ravyn regarded Liz askance. "Did you know he's planning on being a missionary? This summer he's visiting different churches, hoping to gain their support."

"Yeah, I heard something to that effect. The two of you belong to the same church, right?"

"Sort of." Ravyn didn't have time to go into lengthy explanations about the big church forming a spin-off church on the other side of the city.

"Doesn't surprise me that you're religious." Liz leaned sideways against the counter. "I never heard you swear before and you don't slack off like the rest of us."

"That hardly makes me religious, Liz. Anybody can stay busy and refrain from using curse words. What makes me different is . . ." Ravyn paused, realizing she'd never talked about the Lord at work before. While she would never push her faith on others, her coworker was, in fact, probing for answers and at this point in her life, Ravyn felt comfortable enough and ready to share her knowledge. "It's my relationship with Jesus Christ."

An odd expression washed over Liz's tanned and freckled face. "You're one of those fanatics, eh?"

"Hardly. And I make my share of mistakes, so if you're going to suddenly expect me to be perfect, forget it."

"At least you're honest." Liz grinned. "I think that's why I've always liked you. Now back to George — he's going to the Amazon, right?"

"Um, no. Wrong continent. Try Indonesia."

"Oh, that's right. All I could remember was that it's someplace warm."

Ravyn smiled. "No wonder rumors get started around here."

"Yeah, no kidding. Once you hit forty, the memory goes." She took a step closer to Ravyn. "But, speaking of rumors, I found out Carla lied through her teeth about her and George. But you probably knew that already."

"Yes." Ravyn peered back down at the chart again.

"You could have said something. You could have at least told *me*." Liz's voice carried through the partially empty ER. "You should have confronted Carla for lying. She would have deserved it."

"Mark could have confronted her, too." Ravyn lifted her gaze once more and stared into Liz's blue eyes. "But he decided that a softer approach would be more effective, and I've come to realize he was right."

"Yeah, well, we decided on a soft approach, too — none of us are speaking to Carla."

Ravyn pressed her lips together. She refused to get mixed up in the mess.

"But next time you talk to your pal George," Liz said with a lilt in her tone, "tell him that the girls on third in the ER miss him."

"Will do. The news will make his day, I'm sure." Ravyn couldn't help feeling amused.

Then, out of the corner of her eye, she spotted Carla, who pushed a patient's gurney back into his room. Obviously the patient had come from having an x-ray. Ravyn wondered if the younger woman's feelings were hurt now that her coworkers shunned her. But perhaps she didn't care.

Flipping the chart closed, Ravyn checked on Mrs. Hiland, a stroke victim who'd suffered a setback. The neurology team had been summoned to evaluate and treat Mrs. Hiland's symptoms. Ravyn's job was to keep the sweet elderly lady stable until they arrived, and so far so good.

After seeing to her patient's needs, Ravyn exited the room and smacked headlong into Carla.

"I need to talk to you." Carla stuffed her hands into her smock's front pockets. "Can you take a break real quick?"

Ravyn thought it over. "Yeah, I guess now's okay." She thought Carla seemed anxious. "I'll let Liz know I'm leaving."

"Okay, I'll meet you on the smoking deck."

Ravyn went to tell Liz she was taking a break. Then, as promised, she met Carla outside. For the last week, an oppressive heat wave bore down on most of the Midwest, Iowa being no exception. The ER had been full today with people complaining of respiratory problems and other heat-related illnesses. Even now, at two o'clock in the morning, the temperatures were in the eighties and the air felt thick and muggy.

"I've got to show you something." Carla took Ravyn's elbow and steered her under one of the halogen lamps. She lifted her top, revealing her midriff — and something more. A nasty purplish blue bruise spanned her entire left side.

"Ouch." Ravyn winced. "How did you manage that?"

"I fell backward off some bleachers. It was a pretty high fall. I'd been drinking and my friends thought I was dead because when I hit the ground, I knocked myself out cold."

"Did they call an ambulance?"

"No, someone just drove me home."

Ravyn gave her a momentary look of

shock. "They didn't drive you to the hospital?"

"They'd been drinking a lot, too, so they didn't want to get involved."

"Carla!" Ravyn stood arms akimbo. "What kind of friends are those?"

Carla shook her head and thick strands of her blond hair escaped from the clip at her nape. "It doesn't matter. I probably won't see any of them again and, if I do, I won't remember their names or that we even partied together at the park." Carla held her top up higher. "Take a look, Ravyn. Did I break some ribs? I about died, pushing that patient back to the ER from radiology."

"If you're concerned about it, you need to get an x-ray."

"But everyone will talk —"

"Carla, if any coworker reveals your personal health information just to gossip he or she will be in violation of the Federal HIPAA law."

"True, but you know how it goes."

"You have to think about your health first."

After a few more minutes of discussion, Carla finally made the decision to ask her supervisor if she could clock out early. Things weren't terribly busy, so Carla proceeded to check herself into the ER for an examination and x-ray of her midsection. Ravyn managed to work it out so she was Carla's nurse. She escorted her into one of the farthest curtained exam rooms on the opposite side of the nurses' station, so no one else paid much attention to the new admission.

"This is the second time you've come to my rescue," Carla muttered after she'd changed into a white and gray checked gown that wrapped around and tied at the waist. "Mark told me that I could always count on you."

Ravyn realized she'd been hearing the "count on you" comment a lot lately, from Shelley and now Carla, too. But, in truth, people had always relied on Ravyn for as long as she could remember. Her parents, sisters, friends, coworkers — and suddenly she didn't view it as a burdensome thing. She felt flattered. Needed.

"I'm so sick of this life."

"What do you mean?" Ravyn sat on the corner of the linen-covered gurney.

"My life . . ." Carla shook her blond head. "I just wish I could get it together."

"No one can do that for you, Carla."

"I know. But I can't do it alone, either." Tears filled her huge blue eyes, and she tried to blink them back. "I know there are a lot of support groups out there, but that's the problem. Which one do I choose?"

"Would you like to come to a ladies' Bible study with me and my friend Shelley tomorrow night?" The offer bounded out of Ravyn's mouth before she had a chance to really consider it.

"Bible study?"

Ravyn nodded, feeling amazed that twice during the same shift she'd been afforded the chance to share a snippet about her faith. "You'll find the truth about anything you're struggling with in the Bible. It's a great place to start."

Before Carla could answer, the staff physician entered the exam room. Ravyn left so the doctor could examine his patient's injuries, but she made a mental note to give Carla her phone number in case she decided to come to the Bible study. Ravyn had planned to go for Shelley's benefit but realized some time ago that she needed the fellowship and teaching from God's Word as much as anyone else.

Stepping over to the counter where she set down Carla's chart, Ravyn felt awestruck once more. Never before had she witnessed to coworkers. While she had never been ashamed to be a Christian, she'd never gone out of her way to present the Truth, either.

It had been years since God used her as an instrument of His love and goodness, and Ravyn had to admit that it felt good.

NINETEEN

"Over here! Over here!"

Ravyn's gaze followed the voice to the front row where Marky stood waving his arms.

Shelley leaned closer to Ravyn. "Wouldn't you know he found us front row seats? I was hoping for an inconspicuous spot in the back row."

Grinning at the comment and Marky's enthusiasm, Ravyn led the way down the carpeted aisle. Marky had seen her dad's production four times already, not including rehearsals, and she and Shelley had seen it twice, counting tonight — opening night and now the closing Labor Day weekend show. Since Marky had had a hand in the production, Ravyn's folks invited him to the cast party after the show. A more excited ten-year-old couldn't be found in all of Iowa.

"Hurry! Someone might get our seats!"

"Oh, Marky." Shelley said his name on a weary-sounding sigh as they reached him. "I doubt there will be a run on front row seating. Besides, all you'd have to say is that you're saving these seats for your mom and your aunt Ravyn."

Without a reply, the kid turned and sat down. Then he bounced with anticipation in his padded chair.

Shelley deposited a program in his lap and sat beside him. Ravyn took the place next to her. The rest of the row stood empty, and she smiled at Marky's concern that someone might steal their seats if they hadn't acted quickly enough. Typically the Labor Day weekend show wasn't crowded; however, with the college students back on campus now, the small theater might hold a larger than expected audience. Ravyn knew if such a thing occurred it would please her father tenfold.

She stared, unseeing, at the program, which Violet had created on the computer, and thought about how far her dad's summer plays had come over the years. From a tent in the park and hand-typed, one-sheet programs to a beautifully renovated theater on the University of Dubuque campus with central air-conditioning and high-tech brochures that included pictures of each cast member inside. Sure, Dad's plays had been acted out in other theaters before, but sometimes the "theater" was a vacant church or a dark, dingy movie theater ready to close and be demolished. Other times churches lent him their auditoriums. But the time arrived at last when Dad's productions found a fitting home, since the university had offered him the use of this theater indefinitely. Dad was an alum and had, over the years, developed close relationships with several directors on the school's seminary board. They supported his ministry and during the school year Dad would begin teaching a class or two.

Ravyn felt so proud of him.

"Your father is living his dream of serving God in this way," Mark had said during a phone conversation several nights ago. "Your mom has been his perfect *helpmeet* to him."

Ravyn couldn't help the wry grin that tugged at her mouth as she recalled the discussion. She knew Mark was rubbing in the helpmeet part. But she had to admit her cynicism had waned over the summer. She'd seen the power of God in both Shelley's and Carla's lives and realized how complacent, even neglectful, she'd become in her walk with Christ.

In essence, Ravyn had evidenced the power of God in her own life, too.

"This is gonna be good." Marky squirmed in his chair. It seemed he couldn't sit still.

"You've seen this play a dozen times." Shelley shook her head at him in dismay. "Why are you so excited?"

Marky's brown eyes widened with exasperation. "I told you. It's a surprise."

"Oh, good grief." Shelley leaned into Ravyn. "I keep wondering if we should be worried."

"If my dad and your son are in cahoots, I think we should be very worried."

"I hear ya."

They shared a smile and Ravyn guessed her father had told Marky he'd mention his name and thank him publicly for all his hard work this summer. That would explain Marky's insistence on arriving early and claiming front row seats.

The din in the theater began to grow with the number of people. Within a half hour, Ravyn guessed nearly three quarters of the theater had filled. Then, precisely at seven o'clock, the lights in the house dimmed and Al Woods took the stage.

"Good evening, ladies and gentleman." He spoke into the microphone and the audience quieted.

"Thank you for coming tonight. I trust you won't be disappointed with our production." He smiled and Ravyn thought he looked dapper in his dark suit. She marveled at how carefree he appeared while facing a couple hundred pairs of eyes. "Since this is our closing night, I'd like to take a few minutes to thank some very special people. My wife, Zann, for one. Paintress extraordinaire. She created our backdrops and selected the costumes. She also keeps me in line." With a chuckle he turned sideways and extended his arm. "Come on out here, Zann. Take a bow."

Ravyn applauded with the others as her mother waltzed onto the stage, waved to the audience, and then disappeared behind the thick red velveteen curtain.

"After the show, you'll meet our talented cast. At that time, I'll also tell you about our ministry —"

"Anyone sitting here?"

Her attention diverted for the moment, Ravyn gave the gentleman taking the seat beside her an annoyed look. "Um, no," she said in a hushed voice. She wondered why the guy didn't move down one, since there was plenty of room.

She glanced at him again and all at once she noticed his smile, caught the spark of amusement in his gaze, and smelled his zesty cologne.

"Mark!" She couldn't believe her eyes. She kept her tone low since her father was still speaking, but a mix of happiness and disbelief began pumping through her veins. "What are you doing here?"

He placed his arm around her shoulders and gave her a quick kiss. "I wanted to see your dad's play," he whispered. "Well, actually, I wanted to see you."

His words made her want to melt. "When did you get back?"

"A couple of hours ago, but I've been planning to surprise you for about a week. I had a church cancel on me — but I'll tell you about that later."

Ravyn nodded at the same time Shelley nudged her.

"Your dad just called Marky up onstage."

Ravyn grinned and watched as the boy sprang from his seat and made his way up onstage like a pro. When he reached Ravyn's father, he stared into the audience with an awed grin.

"So now, Marky, tell us what happened a few days ago." Dad removed the mike from its stand and held it close to Marky's lips.

"I got saved." His voice shook with mild trepidation.

"Tell our guests here tonight what that word *saved* means."

"Um . . ." Marky seemed stumped. "It means, like *saved,* like firemen save people and stuff."

"Rescued?"

"Yeah." The kid perked up.

"Well, who rescued you and from what were you rescued?"

Ravyn grinned at her father's dramatics.

"Jesus saved me, and I was saved from dying and spending the rest of my whole dead life away from God."

"Dead life? Hmm." Dad folded his arms and cupped his chin, looking thoughtful. "Do you mean eternal life?"

"Yeah, cuz when you die in this life you got another life and you either spend it with God or away from God." Marky used his hands to illustrate the two options. "God is like the sunshine, but the place that's away from God is all dark and nasty."

"Dark and nasty?" Dad shuddered. "Not for me. But, pray tell, how did you get rescued? How can anyone get rescued?"

"Well, it's like this." Marky took the microphone and Ravyn laughed at his sudden boldness. "Everybody's headed for that dark, nasty place because we've all done bad things in our lives. But if you're sorry about doing bad things, then you can get saved by Jesus."

"How?" Dad prompted.

"By asking Him, because Jesus is God's Son and He's got the power."

"A real live Superhero, eh?"

"Yeah, because God can do anything."

"That's right. So how do you feel now that you've been saved?"

"Good."

Ravyn had to laugh at the elementary reply.

"What would you tell others who are doing their own soul-searching?"

"I'd tell 'em to get saved and hurry up. And when it happens, you know it! It's like you can feel yourself get saved on the inside and then, when you open your eyes, everything seems different. Better."

Out of the mouths of babes, Ravyn thought as unexpected tears clouded her vision.

"Wow, that's terrific," Mark whispered near her ear. "He accepted Christ."

"It's a miracle." She smiled at him before glancing at Shelley, who had plump tears dribbling down her narrow face. Reaching under her seat, Ravyn took hold of one of the many tissue boxes strategically placed throughout the theater for times such as these.

She passed the tissues to Shelley. "Marky turned to Christ. He'll be all right now."

"But he's still a little boy who needs his mother," Ravyn reminded her. "Don't go writing yourself off as useless like you've done in the past. Marky needs you."

"Maybe so, but he's a Christian now and as long as chooses to walk with the Lord, he'll never end up in my footsteps."

Dad's voice boomed through the theater. "Well, Marky, that's quite a testimony. Folks," he addressed his audience once more, "this young man has been an enormous help to our summer staff and he's now been adopted into the family of God. Let's give him a big hand."

Ravyn applauded and even stood to give Marky a bear hug when he returned to his seat. "I'm very proud of you, my brother."

His pride and chagrin formed two rosy spots on his suntanned cheeks.

"Way to go, Marky." Mark extended his hand and the child gave his palm a smack.

"Are you surprised, Mom?"

"Am I ever! But I'm happy more than surprised." Shelley's voice was thick with unshed emotion. "Getting saved is the most important decision you'll ever make."

"And you, too." He took his mom's hand and sandwiched it between his two smaller ones. "Mom, if you watch this play tonight you can get saved, too. God doesn't care about all the bad things you've done. He forgives and you can start over."

Overcome with emotion, Ravyn swiped a few tissues from the box still in Shelley's lap. Marky loved his mother so much. The fact had been evident from the first day Ravyn met him. She listened now, wondering if Shelley would explain that she had been saved by grace years ago, but that she'd unfortunately become what the Bible calls in the book of Jeremiah "faithless" and backslidden. Shelley needed God's healing, but as far as Ravyn knew she'd asked Jesus to save her long ago.

Didn't she? Ravyn dabbed her eyes and wiped her nose. Well, that was up to God to judge. Not her. At the present, however, Shelley seemed to have little regard for herself. Instead, she appeared proud and happy with her son for his decision.

"I'll take you out for ice cream after the show, okay? We'll celebrate."

"Okay. Right after the cast party." The joy on Marky's face didn't fade until the lights in the house went down and the curtain opened.

Dry-eyed at last, Ravyn settled in beside Mark. The warmth of his presence and the weight of his arm around her shoulders lent her an assured, secure feeling. She wished this moment would last forever. Everything in the world seemed so indescribably perfect.

The September night air had a nip to it. Ravyn scooted closer to Mark where they glided back and forth on a freestanding wooden swing that had been built on the edge of the park. From their vantage point, they could see the lights from downtown Dubuque sparkling off the Mississippi River.

"Are you cold?" Mark pulled her in tighter, right next to him.

"Not anymore."

He smiled. "Your folks have done a great job with Marky, and Shelley seems to be coming along, too."

"She hasn't missed a day of work all summer."

"I'm impressed. I know you've been keeping me updated on their situations when we've talked on the phone. But to actually see their progress is incredible — and it's all because of your willingness to be used by God."

"No, it's not. God worked in spite of me." Ravyn straightened and looked up into Mark's face. "I've witnessed the power of

God like never before. What's more, I've come to respect my parents' ministry in a way I never thought possible. They hear the Lord's voice and obey Him. It sounds so simplistic, I realize, but to listen for God's still small voice above the din of life with all its trials and temptations isn't easy."

"How well I know that." He bobbed his head as if to emphasize the point.

"I'm ashamed of myself for putting them down for the work they do."

"Hmm. Do you feel that way about overseas missionaries, too?"

Ravyn opened her mouth to reply, but Mark cut her off.

"Before you answer, let me say that I don't know how far across the ocean I'll get at the rate I'm going. I'm only at 27 percent support. After practically knocking myself out at that Bible school program in Wisconsin, the church decided not to sponsor me."

"How disappointing."

"To say the least. Then the next church canceled my visit altogether."

"Well, we both know life's full of setbacks and letdowns, Mark. Why should the ministry be any different that way?"

"I don't know. I guess I just thought it would be. Maybe I've been rather arrogant to think God would hand me my support on a golden platter — just like my aunt and uncle paid my way through med school."

"I think you're being too hard on yourself." She leaned her head against Mark's shoulder again. His long-sleeved chambray shirt felt soft against her face and the side of her arm. "Your aunt and uncle might have paid the school bill, but you worked your backside off and you know it. You earned your MD."

"I worked hard, that's for sure." He kissed her temple. "But I made some phone calls in the last couple of days anyway, and I'm praying about whether to accept a job in an urgent care clinic here in Dubuque. If it's what God wants, I don't mind throwing some of my own money into the support pot."

"Really?" Ravyn turned on the swing to face him. "You're thinking of staying?"

"For now."

"I can't pretend. I'm elated."

"I kind of figured you might be." A half smile tugged at the corner of Mark's mouth. "But please understand that this in no way means I'm giving up my plans for the mission field. I view this as a temporary setback."

"I see it as a blessing. If you were to accept the urgent care position it'll buy us some time."

Mark regarded her askance, wearing a look of mischief. "And what kind of time are you seeking to purchase, madam?" he asked, feigning a French accent.

Ravyn laughed. "You are so crazy."

"That is because I am crazy about you."

He pulled her close to him again, but instead of a kiss, Ravyn felt a buzz when Mark's cell phone vibrated in his shirt pocket.

Startled, she jolted backward. Mark caught her arm before she could topple off the swing.

With one arm around Ravyn, he pulled out his phone. "You've got to stay away from those lattes, girl."

Ravyn caught her breath. "Excuse me. I thought I was being electrocuted by Pepé LePew."

Mark chuckled and answered his phone.

Grinning over the near mishap, Ravyn leaned back in the swing and stared up at the star-studded sky. Her smile faded, however, when she heard the sudden alarm in Mark's voice.

He sat forward, his forearms resting on his knees. "Did you call the paramedics?"

Ravyn moved to the edge of the swing and stared at Mark, wondering what sort of terrible thing had happened.

"Okay, tell them to transport him to Victory Medical Center. I'll meet you there. Did you try to rouse him? Is he breathing? Okay, okay — don't panic. Wait for the paramedics to arrive."

Ravyn's heart sank as she guessed the situation. Mark's uncle had likely suffered another heart attack.

Mark stayed on the line with his great-aunt, trying to calm her, until she announced the emergency medical personnel had arrived. When he finished the call, he confirmed Ravyn's suspicions.

"From what my aunt described, things sound rather grim." Mark's voice sounded tight with emotion as he stood. "I need to get over to the hospital."

"I'm coming with you."

He helped Ravyn off the swing.

"You sure? I have time to drive you home first."

"Nope, I'm positive."

Ravyn slipped her hand into his as they strode to Mark's car. There was no place on earth she'd rather be right now than by his side.

TWENTY

With a cloud of disbelief fogging his mind, Mark stared at his great-uncle's casket. Had it really only been three days ago that Uncle Chet was pronounced dead at the hospital? Everything between then and now seemed a blur of calling friends and family members, meeting with the pastor and funeral director, and picking up relatives at the airport. But now reality struck: Uncle Chet was dead.

A tug on his arm reminded Mark of his aunt Edy. She clung to him as though her legs might not support her if she let go. He told himself to be strong. Aunt Edy needed him. Besides, as a physician, Mark had always been aware that death was a very real part of life. However, the fact hit him on a personal level, and it hit him hard.

The pastor read from the scriptures beneath gloomy skies, which seemed a fitting backdrop for this moment. Unable to concentrate, Mark stared across the gaping red-dish brown earth and spotted Ravyn. Wearing somber garb, she stood alongside her family with Shelley and her son. Mark would have liked to feel Ravyn's presence beside him today. But his immediate family had arrived from New Hampshire and they pressed in around him.

Ravyn. He didn't know how he would have managed without her these past couple of days. She had been a big help in consoling his aunt. Mark only hoped Ravyn understood that his neglect of her hadn't been intentional.

As if he'd spoken the illogical thought aloud, she glanced up and met his gaze. He saw only empathy in her expressive dark eyes. If he hadn't realized it before, he did now; he loved Ravyn.

She gave him a little smile before lowering her gaze. Mark, too, bowed his head as the pastor began to read the Twenty-third Psalm.

" 'The Lord is my shepherd; I shall not be in want. . . .' "

The graveside service ended and Mark lost sight of Ravyn, although he knew he'd catch up with her at some point. He focused on his duties at hand and helped Aunt Edy across the small country cemetery. They reached the parking lot, and he helped her into the car before walking around and climbing in behind the wheel.

"I invited the Woodses over to the small gathering at the house." Aunt Edy smoothed down the skirt of her black dress before she snapped her seat belt into place. "I didn't think you'd mind."

Mark started the car's engine. "Of course I don't."

"About time the two families meet each other."

"I agree." He sent his great-aunt a small smile and pulled out of the parking slip.

Silence spanned the next several minutes.

"Chet was very proud of you. He left a provision for you in his will. It's in the form of a life insurance policy and its sum will take care of any funds you're lacking in church support."

"Let's talk about this later, all right?"

"Yes." Aunt Edy's voice sounded strained. "I just thought you should know about the money. Chet wanted very much to help you realize your goals to serve the Lord on the mission field and that policy will help you get there."

"And what about you?" Mark braked for a stoplight and turned to his great-aunt. Her fawn-colored hair curled out from beneath the round black hat she wore. "I need to know you'll be well provided for."

"Oh, yes, I'll be fine." She held her hanky to her nose. "Chet made sure of it."

Mark's heart broke as she began to weep. He reached over and touched her shoulder and felt it shake beneath his palm. He felt like sobbing himself. It was hard to believe Uncle Chet wouldn't be at home when they arrived.

But of course, he was home — with the Lord in His eternal home in heaven.

Aunt Edy composed herself. "Nothing would make me happier than to see you marry Ravyn Woods and set off to Indonesia. She's a special young woman. Such a sensitive soul. She's been a comfort to me in the last couple of days, and she took in Shelley Jenkins and her boy. Why, she also brings that other young lady to our Bible study."

"Carla?"

"Yes, that's her."

"Aunt Edy, you don't have to convince me of Ravyn's big-hearted attributes. I've seen them for myself."

In spite of his comment, Mark's anguish mounted. He only had to recall how pleased Ravyn had been when he'd mentioned the position at the urgent care clinic. He hated

261

the thought of disappointing her now. Worse, he didn't want to lose her altogether.

Nevertheless, he knew that if God provided the funds by way of Uncle Chet's will, then he had to go.

"How can you eat tacos after all that food at the Dariens' this afternoon?" Shelley pulled out a chair and sat down at the kitchen table beside Ravyn.

"I'm starving. I didn't get a chance to eat. I was too busy meeting Mark's family." She sipped her cola. "All his sisters look alike. I hope I remember their names."

"They seem very nice." Shelley smiled and helped herself to a nacho chip, then dipped it in the warm and spicy cheese sauce. "His brothers are good-looking men. Too bad for me they're all married."

Ravyn grinned at the remark since her mouth was too full of taco to reply. But all kidding aside, she'd notice how Mark's siblings went out of their way to befriend her. It went without saying that she and Mark were officially serious about each other.

"For a funeral gathering, it was actually an enjoyable afternoon."

Again, Ravyn bobbed out an answer.

Shelley tipped her head, looking rather

bookish in her navy dress with its gold belt and her hair clipped up. "So why don't you marry Mark and live happily ever after?"

"Well, for starters," Ravyn said, swallowing her last bite, "he hasn't proposed. But, yeah, that is the goal."

Shelley laughed under her breath and ate another tortilla chip. She'd gained some weight this summer and didn't appear so sickly thin anymore. "I'll bet he'd pop the question in a heartbeat if he knew you'd say yes."

"I don't know if I'd say yes. That's why Mark and I are dating."

"Smart aleck. You forget I live with you. I know that missionary thing is holding you back."

"Not anymore. Mark might be the newest MD at the urgent care clinic across from the medical center."

"Oh, right. I sort of heard mutterings about that this afternoon. But I also heard it's not a done deal."

"It's not," Ravyn conceded, although she had been praying to that end. She had to wonder, too, how Mark's great-uncle's death might figure into his decision. She hoped he'd want to remain in Dubuque for his great-aunt's sake.

Shelley glanced at the clock on the microwave and stood. Strolling into the living room, she instructed Marky to turn off the TV and get ready for bed. After a few whines and complaints, he did as his mother asked and Shelley returned to her place at the table.

"This afternoon I saw a lot of people I hadn't seen in a decade or more. I felt overwhelmed at the flood of memories. I kept thinking about my parents. They were well-off financially and I was an only child and yet, they didn't love me the way I longed to be loved. I was a trophy of their marriage and only something to be seen and not heard. But in actuality, I think I would have done anything if my dad would have chosen to spend time with me rather than play golf or attend the men's club at church or go off on any number of his favorite recreations away from home."

Ravyn didn't reply. By now she could sense when Shelley needed to talk and rid herself of the past demons that continually haunted her.

"When we were kids, I used to relish going over to your house. Your folks might not have wallowed in material wealth, but they loved you and I felt that love through you. That's why I hung around."

"My parents liked it when you hung

around because then they got two baby-sitters for the price of one."

"Ulterior motives, eh?"

"Uh-huh."

"Well, they still loved you girls. And now Mark loves you, too, Ravyn."

She lifted her gaze and peered at her friend. "Think so? *Love* is a strong word."

"I watched him today. His whole face lit up when you entered the room. He didn't notice anyone else. It was as if he totally zoned out and focused only on you."

"Really?" Ravyn felt a jolt of pleasure at the news. She hadn't noticed.

"When you weren't around, Mark's eyes searched you out — even while he was talking with other people." Shelley sighed. "I found it quite aggravating while trying to have a discussion with him."

Ravyn laughed.

Shelley glanced at the tabletop, running the side of her fingernail along the wood grain. "You are loved, Ravyn, and you don't know how lucky you are."

Ravyn reached out and set her hand on her friend's forearm. "Shelley, please don't —"

"I'm not saying this to make you feel bad. I'm telling you this, Rav, so you don't throw away something wonderful between you and

Mark just because things don't stack up according to the way you've planned."

She retracted her hand as an inner wall of defense began to rise.

"Don't be angry with me. Hear me out, okay? Mark might be that one guy — the one chance at love you'll never have again. If you let it go you might regret it forever. I mean, if it were me in your place, I'd follow the guy to Timbuktu."

Ravyn held back a retort. Her mother and Teala had told her much the same thing. If you love someone, you ought to be able to follow him to the ends of the earth. But what close friends and well-intentioned family members didn't take into account were Ravyn's hard-earned career and her own plans for the future. Why couldn't Mark follow *her*?

A bit miffed, Ravyn collected all the wrappers from her fast-food supper and stuffed them into the paper bag. "You're forgetting that Mark has yet to mention the word *love* around me."

"He's probably scared. Think about it. Would you want to bare your heart to someone you thought might dump you if you decided to be a missionary?"

Ravyn tensed. "Shelley! You make me sound like I'm a shallow person. I'm not."

"Of course you're not. Look at all you've done for me and for Marky. Where would we be if it weren't for you?" She stood. "I didn't mean to offend you. But now I have to go tuck a certain ten-year-old into bed. He's got school tomorrow."

A forgiving smile played on Ravyn's lips, although as she watched Shelley leave the room, she couldn't seem to shake off everything she'd said.

In fact, the comments lingered in her mind all through the night. She thought and prayed and prayed some more.

Lord, what do I do if Mark makes the decision to go overseas?

The answer boomeranged back to her soul.

Trust and obey.

A hard rain splattered against the window as Ravyn stared out across the empty tennis courts. She stifled a yawn and turned back to Mark. He had called a half hour ago saying he needed to speak with her, that it was important. Now seemed the perfect time with Shelley at work and Marky at school. But, after working all night, Ravyn felt exhaustion creeping into her senses. The fact that Mark seemed at a loss for words only frustrated her.

She regarded him for several long moments as he sat on the edge of the sofa, which had doubled as her bed since Shelley moved in. His arms dangled over his knees. His expression looked solemn. In a word, he looked like one miserable man.

"Are you sure I can't get you something? I could make some lunch if you're hungry."

"No, that's okay." He stood and shoved his hands into the pockets of his tan casual trousers. He cleared his throat. "I'm glad you had a fun time shopping with my mom and sisters the other day."

"I did." She narrowed her gaze. "But that's not what you came over to discuss, is it? Our shopping trip?"

"No." He gave a slight wag of his head. "I'm working up to the real issue."

"Well, you're making me nervous. Maybe you should just spit it out and get it over with."

"Easy for you to say."

Ravyn wasn't amused by the quip. "Is it about your aunt?" She knew Mark had been preoccupied this last week with various legal matters. "Is it your family? They made it back to New Hampshire okay, didn't they?"

"Everyone's fine." Mark took a few steps toward her. "Look, I just wanted you to know I turned down the job at the clinic."

"Okay."

Ravyn felt a tad perplexed. She didn't know why he'd feel hesitant about telling her that, unless it meant —

Reality slammed into her. "Y–you're headed for that little island off of Indonesia, aren't you?"

"Yes, I am." Mark's brown eyes seemed so sad. "I'm sorry, Ravyn. I know this is what God wants me to do and where He wants me to go."

"Then why are you sorry?" She moved toward him. "You're trusting and obeying God. You're honorable and committed."

"Thanks, but —"

"Don't tell me you're leaving tomorrow!"

"No." A rueful grin tugged at the corner of his mouth. "In January. Like I planned. I need to do some healing after my uncle's untimely death and I want to make sure my aunt's going to be okay."

"Understandable and . . . very gallant."

"You're very complimentary this morning, Ravyn, and you're, um, taking this a lot better than I expected. I don't know if that makes me feel good or bad." He flashed a bit of a smile before a stony expression washed over his expression again. "What I want to know is, where does my decision leave us?"

Questions crowded her thoughts. Couldn't he tell she loved him? Why didn't he ask her to marry him? But then she recalled what Shelley had said about a guy not wanting to bare his heart if he thought he'd get dumped. Ravyn realized she had some explaining to do.

"Mark, I know I haven't been very supportive in the past of missionaries in general, but after a lot of dialogue with God, I've reconsidered."

"Oh?" He placed his hands on his hips and his expression seemed to soften.

Ravyn inched her way closer. "The truth is I love you. I think I've loved you since I was sixteen. I wish you wouldn't leave Dubuque, but if that's how the Lord is directing you, and it obviously is, then I want to go with you."

"You — what?" He looked stunned. "Wait a second. Let me get this straight. Are you saying you'll give up your nursing career and your future plans to go overseas with me?"

"Yes, that's exactly what I'm saying." Suddenly it all seemed so very simple. "All my well-laid plans won't mean anything if I'm unhappy. Besides, they're *my* plans and they have been all along. They're not God's plans."

Mark closed the distance between them and cupped her face with his hands. He urged her gaze into his. "Are you sure, Ravyn?"

"I'm sure. It means a lot to me that you're willing to follow the Lord and not cave in to external pressures. No matter what happens I'll be able to rest in the knowledge that your utmost desire is to walk with Christ." Tears blurred her vision. "Like my dad."

A smile grew wide across his face. "You'd have to marry me."

"Oh, well, forget it," she teased with an upward flick of her gaze.

His laugh filled the living room and a moment later, her feet left the carpeted floor as Mark twirled her around before wrapping her in a snug embrace.

"Of course I'll marry you, Mark." Ravyn felt his lips graze her temple.

"I love you."

"I know." With her head pressed against his heart, she smiled.

"You're perfect for me. You challenge and encourage me." He gently pushed her back and stared down into her eyes. "God filled my prescription for love — with you."

Ravyn felt special, cherished, and, yes, loved. And while it wasn't the proposal of marriage she'd imagined, she'd never experienced such joy. She knew at that precise moment she'd made the right decision.

And now she was about to seal it with a kiss.

EPILOGUE

"Okay, everyone, look this way and smile!"

The photographer snapped several shots while the wedding party stood poised on the deep-red carpeted steps of the church's platform. Scarlet-leafed poinsettias were lined up in a row at their feet. The plants contrasted in seasonal fashion with the evergreen-colored dresses worn by the six bridesmaids. Mark and his groomsmen looked their dashing best in black tuxedos, although Ravyn's gaze never strayed beyond her handsome husband. Christmas had always been one of her favorite holidays and now the celebration carried with it an extra special blessing; she'd just married the man she loved.

Ravyn pressed in a little closer to her husband.

A few more pictures were taken. Minutes later, the wedding party disbanded and made its way downstairs for the small reception, the happy bride and groom included. The pastor had agreed to marry Ravyn and Mark in the larger, founding church in order to accommodate the many guests.

As they entered the spacious fellowship area decorated with white paper wedding bells and streamers, family members and friends cheered. Then Ravyn and Mark cut their wedding cake amid more applause and pictures.

"Wow, I hardly recognize you two without your scrubs on," Liz said minutes later, after taking a sip of punch. "But I'll say this much, you make a perfect couple."

Ravyn felt Mark tighten his hold around her waist. She smiled. "We think so, too."

Liz set her punch down on a nearby table and gave both Ravyn and Mark a hug. "I'll sure miss you two. Make sure you e-mail me and keep me updated on what's happening overseas."

"We will," Mark promised.

Several other coworkers expressed their congratulations and then Carla approached them. Her cheeks held a rosy hue that matched her two-piece skirt and sweater.

She wrapped Ravyn in a sisterly embrace. "You look beautiful and the ceremony made me cry. It was so lovely." She took Mark's hand and gave it a congratulatory squeeze.

"And guess what just happened? Mrs. Darien asked if I'd move in with her and I said yes."

"I'm so glad." Ravyn felt additional tears of happiness spring to her eyes. Carla hadn't been in a good living situation for a long time. Her roommates liked to party in irresponsible, even dangerous ways.

"Aunt Edy discussed the matter with Ravyn and me," Mark said. "We were all for it from the beginning. I think you and my aunt will be an encouragement to each other."

"Thanks. She's pretty cool for an older lady."

Ravyn smiled and then more guests captured her and Mark's attention.

Finally Shelley made her way to them. Marky sat at a nearby table, eating cake and joking with other kids his age.

"I'll never forgive you for stealing my roommate." She flicked a teasing glance at Mark and hugged Ravyn. "I'm going to miss her."

"Well," Mark answered with a wry grin, "according to my aunt, wedding bells might be in your future, too."

"Oh, I don't know about that." Shelley actually blushed. "Trevor's a nice guy and everything and Marky certainly likes him, but . . ." She glanced over her shoulder and Ravyn followed her gaze to the stocky-framed man with light brown hair refilling his punch glass. "We'll see."

Ravyn had a hunch Mark was right: marriage lurked around the corner for Shelley. Shelley and Trevor had met during a junior high outing at church about the same time she'd found a new job as an administrative assistant at one of the city's many foundries. With the better salary, Shelley had decided she could assume Ravyn's monthly mortgage payments and take care of the condo while Ravyn and Mark were overseas.

"Oh, Ravyn, where would I be without you?" Shelley gave her another hug. "Sometimes I'm scared that you're leaving. I've relied on you for five months."

"And now it's time to rely on God. He's always with you."

"I know."

"Besides, my parents are just a phone call away."

"My aunt, too," Mark added.

Shelley nodded.

A moment later, Ravyn's father's voice commanded everyone's attention. "A special toast to the bride and groom," he said, lifting his punch glass. "May your ministry together be all God intended from the beginning of time, and may your lives be filled with special blessings."

"Yes, like lots of grandchildren!" Mark's mother exclaimed.

Everyone cheered and Ravyn rode out her wave of embarrassment with a smile. Then she looked up at Mark and he gazed into her eyes with unabashed love and desire before kissing her. Applause and laughter filled the room, and at that precise moment Ravyn knew she'd live nothing short of happily ever after.

The employees of Thorndike Press hope you have enjoyed this Large Print book. All our Thorndike, Wheeler, and Kennebec Large Print titles are designed for easy reading, and all our books are made to last. Other Thorndike Press Large Print books are available at your library, through selected bookstores, or directly from us.

For information about titles, please call:
(800) 223-1244

or visit our Web site at:
http://gale.cengage.com/thorndike

To share your comments, please write:
Publisher
Thorndike Press
295 Kennedy Memorial Drive
Waterville, ME 04901